Praise for the novels of Elizabeth Mansfield

The Girl with the Persian Shawl

"Popular Regency author Mansfield gives readers another classic treat with this charmingly sweet romance, a Regency notable for its polished writing and gleaming wit." —*Booklist*

"Elizabeth Mansfield has long been one of the most popular writers of Regency romances. . . . *The Girl with the Persian Shawl* should appeal to Mansfield's many fans as well as to those who enjoy traditional Regency romances." —*The Romance Reader*

"A delightful traditional Regency. Kate is a wonderfully strong character in the tradition of Jane Austen's Emma. . . . Ms. Mansfield has provided a charming cast of secondary characters. . . . For anyone who enjoys the Regency period, *The Girl with the Persian Shawl* is a must read!" —The Best Reviews

"A delightful journey through Regency England, with engaging characters and an entertaining plot. The dialogue is bright and realistic, and the secondary characters add a lot of humor. . . . This book is a must read for Regency lovers." —Romance Reviews Today

"Charming. . . . Readers will enjoy this witty relationship romp." —AllReaders.com

continued . . .

Miscalculations

"A light and enjoyable book. It has humor, romance, and a bit of intrigue. Readers who have never read a . . . Regency romance could not find a better author to introduce them to the joys of the [genre]."

—*The Romance Reader*

"Her best to date . . . a captivating plot that brings the era to life. Entertaining [and] appealing."

—BookBrowser

Matched Pairs

"Elizabeth Mansfield's tale of lasting friendship and misplaced jealousy is well done. The characters are so enchanting, you can't wait to turn the next page."

—*Affaire de Coeur*

Poor Caroline

"Ms. Mansfield proves why she is one of the enduring names in romance with this sparkling traditional Regency tale, brimming with lively dialogue and charming characters." —*The Paperback Forum*

"Elizabeth Mansfield is renowned for delighting readers with deliciously different Regency romances. A true comedy of manners that results in a diamond-of-the-first-order book."

—*Affaire de Coeur*

An Encounter with Venus

Elizabeth Mansfield

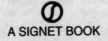

A SIGNET BOOK

SIGNET
Published by New American Library, a division of
Penguin Group (USA) Inc., 375 Hudson Street,
New York, New York 10014, U.S.A.
Penguin Books Ltd, 80 Strand,
London WC2R 0RL, England
Penguin Books Australia Ltd, 250 Camberwell Road,
Camberwell, Victoria 3124, Australia
Penguin Books Canada Ltd, 10 Alcorn Avenue,
Toronto, Ontario, Canada M4V 3B2
Penguin Books (N.Z.) Ltd, Cnr Rosedale and Airborne Roads,
Albany, Auckland 1310, New Zealand

Penguin Books Ltd, Registered Offices:
80 Strand, London WC2R 0RL, England

First published by Signet, an imprint of New American Library,
a division of Penguin Group (USA) Inc.

First Printing, December 2003
10 9 8 7 6 5 4 3 2 1

 REGISTERED TRADEMARK—MARCA REGISTRADA

Printed in the United States of America

To the eyes of a miser,
    a guinea is far more beautiful than the sun . . .
The tree, which moves some to tears of joy,
    is in the eyes of others only a green thing
    that stands in the way.
As a man is, so he sees.

—William Blake

Prologue

Ten years earlier, when he was seventeen, George Frobisher had caught a glimpse of Miss Olivia Henshaw naked. It was a moment he never forgot.

He'd been granted leave from Cambridge to attend his sister's wedding, which was to be held at Leyton Abbey, the groom's country estate in Yorkshire. He did not usually enjoy attending weddings, nor did he like having to leave school so close to examination week, but Felicia, six years older than he, was his only sibling, and he was very fond of her. He therefore tried to make the best of it for her sake.

While dressing for the ceremony, he realized he was missing a stud for his shirtfront. Since the valet his host had provided for him was elderly and slow, he decided to go himself to find his father's bedroom and borrow a stud. The Abbey was a warren of crenellated hallways and dark passages, and trying to find his way, he'd passed a slightly opened doorway. The light from the doorway spilled out into the corridor and drew his eyes. And there, right in his line of sight, was this vision of exquisite loveliness. A young woman was stepping from a shallow tub of steaming water, her body rosy from the heat, and her arms outstretched to receive a towel that an unseen maidservant was handing her. Her skin was smooth as ivory and glistened with the rivulets of water that flowed down her body. Her wet hair clung to a shapely neck. Her shoulders were gently sloped, her arms softly rounded, and the outline of her hips led down in a luscious, unbroken curve to her breathtaking thighs. Above a slim waist were two perfectly shaped breasts, made even more delicious by the single drop of water clinging to one pink nipple. She was a work of art, an Italian masterpiece, a Venus emerging from a steamy sea!

He stood there staring, mesmerized, his seventeen-year-old self shaken, entranced, overwhelmed. Only when she'd stepped out of the tub and passed from his line of sight did he recover his equilibrium.

As soon as he could move again, he ran down the hallway to his sister's room and, ignoring her abigail's remonstrances, burst in on her. "Felicia," he demanded breathlessly, "who's the person occupying the bedroom three doors down on the left?"

His sister, at this moment being helped into her underskirts, glared at him. "Really, Georgie," she said in disgust, "why on earth must you make a to-do on the most important day of my life? Why do you want to know?"

"Never mind why," he demanded. "Just tell me!"

Felicia shrugged in surrender. "Let me think. Third door down? That would be Livy. Olivia Henshaw. One of my very best friends. And if you won't tell me why you want to know her name, just get out of here and let me dress."

"Very well, I'm going," he said, adding over his shoulder as he scooted out the door, "but be sure to make me known to her, will you?"

However, the introduction was never made. When he returned to his room, he found the valet waiting with an urgent message from his school. His closest friend, Bernard Tretheway, had been thrown from a horse and had badly injured his back. George returned to Cambridge at once.

In the ten years since that day, he'd not seen nor heard anything of Miss Olivia Henshaw. Until today.

One

George would be the first to admit that a momentary glimpse of a Venus ten years earlier was not an important event in the larger scheme of things. After all, the ensuing decade had been filled with many more significant occurrences. From that very day, when he'd returned to Cambridge to find that Bernard had lost the use of his legs, the decade had been full of meaningful experiences. After graduation, George had taken a flat with Bernard in London to help him adjust to life on crutches. Then, a year later, with Bernard's insistence that he could manage on his own, George had joined Lord Wellington as an officer in the Spanish campaign and saw firsthand the devastations of war. After Waterloo, he and Bernard had become involved in politics, actively engaging in the struggle for parliamentary reform. Then his father had died, and George had succeeded to his title: Earl of Chadleigh. There hadn't been time to dwell on so insignificant an event as a glimpse of a naked lady.

Yet even now, at the much more mature age of twenty-seven, and even after seeing many unclad females of varying degrees of beauty, he could still close his eyes and bring to mind that momentary sight. And the memory of it could still set his blood astir. That was why he agreed to attend a house party his sister was giving at the Abbey in Yorkshire.

His sister's party was the type of social event he usually avoided, but Felicia had traveled down to London expressly to coax him to attend. Even so, he was, at first, adamant in his refusal. He knew why she tried so hard to entice him. Not only did she need as many gentlemen as she could find to please her female guests, but she was particularly eager to marry her brother off to one of her many unwed friends, all of whom considered George Frobisher, the Earl of Chadleigh, a most desirable catch. George, however, had no intention of being caught. "When I'm ready for wedlock," he'd told his sister more than once, "I'll find my own bride."

Nevertheless, over a sumptuous luncheon at Fenton's hotel, Felicia kept insisting that he come. "I promise you, Georgie, that on this occasion you'll have a lovely time."

From across the table, George eyed his sister suspiciously. She was looking particularly appealing this afternoon. She'd worn a feathered bonnet with a small, round brim that accented her full cheeks and only partially hid her auburn curls, making her look—as she well knew!— much younger than her thirty-three years. Her large blue eyes were looking across at him so appealingly that he had to stiffen himself to refuse her. But he was determined to do just that. He knew he was an easygoing fellow who found it hard to refuse any request from family or friends . . . in fact, he was aware that the men at his club referred to him affectionately as a soft touch. But when it came to fending off predatory females, he was determinedly firm. And predatory females would certainly be present at Felicia's house party. "You don't need me, Felicia," he said as he speared a piece of pickled salmon with his fork. "You always have a crush."

"It won't be a crush, this time," she promised. "There will only be ten at table. It will be such fun! I have costumes for an amusing tableau, we're to have a tour of the old church at Rudston—it has a genuine pagan monolith on the grounds!—and my dear Leyton is planning a shooting party—"

George cut off her enthusiastic recital. "I've always

wondered, Felicia, why you insist on calling your husband by his family name. You never call me by mine."

"Really, Georgie, I can scarcely be expected to call my baby brother Frobisher."

"But surely a husband is a more intimate relation than a brother."

"It's his given name, you see. Montague. He hates it. But don't try to distract me, dearest. I so want you to come! It will be a wonderful weekend, really it will!"

George would not be moved. "You know how I hate to play the extra man at your dinner table," he told her flatly. "The ladies you ask are invariably annoying."

"That's not true. You seem to find fault with all the women you meet. If you didn't, you'd be wed by this time."

"There may be some truth in that. Most of the young ladies I come across are too compliant and mawkish, too trivial-minded or too aggressively flirtatious."

"Compliant? Trivial? Aggressively flirtatious?" Felicia studied him curiously. "What do you mean by that? Would you describe my friends that way? Too sweet or too shallow or too bold?"

"Most of them. Do you remember your birthday fete last year? One of your friends—I can't remember her name . . . the tall one with the frizzled hair that she tied up on one side of her head—"

"Do you mean Lillian Plante?"

"That's the one. She drew me out on the terrace and actually dared me to offer for her, the silly chit."

"It wouldn't have hurt you to have done it," Felicia retorted. "It's about time you were married. But Lillian isn't coming this time. She's gotten herself betrothed. I'm only having Elaine Whitmore and—"

"Whitmore? Whitmore?" George tried to bring her to mind. "Is she the one with the high-pitched giggle?"

Felicia shook her head. "You haven't yet met her, but she is, I promise you, the very loveliest creature. I've also asked Beatrice Rossiter and—"

"Ah, Beatrice Rossiter! *There's* a treat," George

scoffed. "Speaking of trivial-mindedness, no sooner do you say your how-de-dos to her than she begins her aimless chattering and never stops."

"You mustn't mind that. She only does it to hide her shyness."

"Indeed? Shy, is she?" He chuckled scornfully. "Shy as a rooster at dawn, I'd say. One wonders how she manages to snatch a breath."

"You're being unkind," his sister accused, but without real bite. Defending Beatrice was not her objective; getting her brother to come to her party was. "But, Georgie, please, stop finding fault. Let me tell you who else will be with us. Let's see, Lord and Lady Stoneham, and Leyton's friends, the Thomsett brothers, Horace and Algy. And Livy, of course."

"Livy?" he asked. "Who's Livy."

"Olivia Henshaw. An old friend from school. You needn't trouble about her."

Olivia Henshaw! The mere sound of that almost-forgotten name brought him on instant alert, in the same way that, when he was on bivouac with the army, a cracking twig would bring him suddenly awake. He felt his whole body stiffen inside, but the only outer movement he made was the lifting of one eyebrow. "No?" he managed to ask. "Why needn't I trouble about her?"

"She's two years older than I—much too old for you."

But George wasn't really listening. He was seeing in his mind's eye a Venus emerging from a tub. The vision was so real that his heart clenched. It occurred to him with a shock that he wanted nothing more than to attend his sister's house party after all.

"Please, Georgie," Felicia was pleading, but without much hope, "I've three unattached females and only two single men, the Thomsetts. I need you! Do be a darling and come this once!"

"Very well," he said in what his sister thought was an abrupt and utterly surprising capitulation, "I'll come to your blasted house party. Just this once."

Felicia gave a little scream of delight, jumped up from

her chair, ran round the table, and threw her arms about his neck. "Oh, you darling!" she cried. "I'm so glad!"

George scarcely noticed the embrace. All he could think of was that—at last!—he was going to meet his Venus face-to-face.

Two

After leaving Felicia, George strolled along Regent Street toward Chadleigh House, swinging his walking stick jauntily—too jauntily, perhaps, for a man of his age and position. But he couldn't help it. His blood was bubbling with a boyish sense of anticipation, an excitement he hadn't experienced in years. How could he go home to a quiet house when he felt this inner churning? He changed his direction, deciding instead to drop in at Bernard's rooms.

He found Bernard at his desk going over his notes for a speech he was to give that evening at Brooks' club. "I wasn't expecting you this afternoon," Bernard said, turning his wheelchair about and looking up in surprise. "Didn't you say you'd pick me up about eight?"

"Yes, but I wanted to tell you about my luncheon with my sister," George explained. "I agreed to go to her party at the Abbey on the fourteenth."

"The fourteenth?" Bernard's eyes widened in alarm. "But that's right before the ball!"

"A full week before," George countered. "I'll leave on Thursday. I've only promised for the weekend. I can be back on Monday, in plenty of time for a ball on Wednesday night."

"You can't be sure of that." Bernard wheeled himself in nervous agitation across the room to where George stood. "What if there's a storm? Or an accident to your carriage? Damnation, George, you know how important the Renwoods' ball is to me!"

George knew. Bernard was struggling with feelings of love for the first time since their school days. He'd at long last found a lady who attracted him and who'd not shown revulsion at his crippled legs. Women did not often take to Bernard, either when he was standing upright on his crutches or seated in his wheelchair. He was not a handsome fellow to begin with, having a too-large nose and thick, bushy hair that he could not keep smoothed down. In addition, his accident had bent his six-foot two-inch frame into a somewhat hunchbacked shape. George, of course, believed the ladies to be short-sighted. In George's view, Bernard was perfectly prepossessing—his expression intelligent, his eyes bright, his wit keen. But for most ladies, he had little physical appeal, and ironically, on the few occasions when one did find him pleasing, he found reasons not to like her. Until he met Harriet.

Harriet Renwood was a sweet creature with a soft voice, a warm smile, and a pair of melting brown eyes. She'd sat down beside Bernard at a recent dinner party and engaged him in conversation for the entire evening. She'd even refused two other gentlemen when they'd interrupted to ask her to dance. Her manner had been so encouraging to Bernard's hopes that he'd been top-over-tail ever since. When, a few days later, he and George had each received an invitation to the very exclusive Renwood ball, Bernard was quite beside himself. George fully understood why. Because of his incapacity, Bernard was seldom invited to balls; therefore, this invitation was, to his mind, proof of the lady's interest in him. He could hardly wait for the event to take place.

George studied his friend with sincere sympathy. "I know what it means to you, Bernard. I fully intend to be there. But if, as you say, something should occur to prevent me, it shouldn't matter. Dash it all, man, you don't need me with you. If that dinner party the other night is any indication, Harriet Renwood will not leave your side all evening."

"At a ball given by one's own mother, a girl wouldn't be permitted to spend the evening exclusively with one gentleman, even if she might wish to. She'd have to fill at least *some* of her dance card. And when she does get up to dance, what shall I do with myself without your company? I'll have to stand about on the sidelines, leaning on my crutches like a poor, pathetic mooncalf."

"What rot!" George exclaimed. "As if there won't be a dozen fellows to surround you, eager to argue about your views on the corn laws, to say nothing of the elderly ladies who always flutter about to mother you. How many times have *I* had to stand about on the sidelines like a lost soul while *you* were otherwise occupied?"

"Stand about on the sidelines, do you?" his friend scoffed. "I have yet to see the day when you don't have your pick of any of the ladies present."

George waved away the comment. "Seriously, Bernard, you needn't let a ball frighten you. A man who can speak his views before packed audiences at every club in town can certainly handle himself at a mere ball."

"This is not a *mere* ball. My *heart* is at stake. Damnation, George, I'll need your support that night of all nights!"

"Very well, you'll have it. I'll be back in time, I promise."

Bernard eyed him dubiously. "I don't understand why you agreed to go to the Abbey in the first place. You've never enjoyed your sister's social events above half."

"This time I have a special interest. I understand that one of her guests is to be someone I've very much wished to meet. I've wished it for a long, long time."

"Oh?" Bernard raised a curious eyebrow. "Who is that? A lady?"

"Yes," George said with a grin. "A lovely lady."

"Very lovely?"

"The loveliest."

"Do I know of her?"

"No."

Bernard peered up at his friend with knotted brows. "How is it you've never told me of her?"

"I've never met her, you see."

"Never met her?" Bernard shook his head in confusion. "Then how do you know she's so very lovely?"

"I didn't say I'd never *seen* her," George explained. "I only said I never *met* her."

Bernard stared at his friend in utter perplexity. "*What?*"

"Don't gape at me as if I'd suddenly grown an extra nose," George said, laughing. "I caught a glimpse of her once, that's all."

Bernard threw up his hands. "This is all too much for me," he muttered. "You're not behaving like yourself at all." He wheeled himself about, returned to his desk, and began rummaging through his papers. "That mere 'glimpse' hasn't so greatly overset you as to cause you to change your plans for this evening, has it?"

George snorted. "Good God, no."

"Then you'll still be picking me up?"

"Yes, of course." George started toward the door. "Eight sharp."

"George?" Bernard asked with an urgent quiver in his voice. "You did mean what you said before?"

George paused in the doorway. "What was that?"

"That you'll be back from your Yorkshire trip on time, no matter what?"

"I'll be back," George assured him. "You have my word."

Bernard lowered his head to his work again. "I only hope that mysterious lady will make your untimely trip to Yorkshire worth your while," he muttered lugubriously.

Feeling a bit foolish about the entire matter, George could only answer, "I hope so, too."

Three

*B*ernard may have felt that the trip to Yorkshire was untimely, but to George the time seemed long overdue. In all the years since his first glimpse of his "Venus," he'd never imagined that he would actually meet her. She'd become, in his mind, a dream, a vision, an ideal beyond reach. Now, suddenly, she was becoming real. A meeting was imminent, and he found himself unwontedly eager for it. Nevertheless, this boyish impatience surprised him. After all, he was a twenty-seven-year-old man-of-the-world, wasn't he?

You're no longer a green lad, he cautioned himself all during the ride to Yorkshire, *so stop behaving like one!* But the trip, which took only seven hours instead of the expected eight, seemed endless to George. He'd chosen to drive his phaeton and pair, and at one point he caught himself urging his matched bays to race at an almost breakneck speed. His young tiger, Timmy, wondering what maggot had gotten into his lordship's head to make him abuse his favorite horses in that manner, cried out a warning. George got hold of himself and made the bays slow down. *I'm no longer a seventeen-year-old,* he reminded himself. It was foolish to give such significance to what had been a mere moment of his life. But he couldn't be blamed—could he?—for feeling some excitement at having been given a second chance to learn what might have happened if that moment had not been cut short.

They arrived at Leyton Abbey at sundown. George, windblown and disheveled as he was, leaped from the box, threw the reins to the tiger, and ran up the front steps. His sister was on hand to welcome him, but he gave her only a quick, wordless embrace and dashed past her to the drawing room without so much as a pause to remove his driving gloves.

The room was completely deserted.

He swung about to his sister, who'd followed him down the hall. "Where are your guests?" he demanded in frustration.

"Judging from your eagerness to meet them," she said in surprise, "one would think I was entertaining the Prince Regent."

"Never mind Prinny. Where are your guests?" he insisted.

"Prinny sent regrets," she retorted sarcastically. "The rest are dressing for dinner, of course." She pushed him toward the stairway. "And so must you. Really, Georgie, you're behaving most peculiarly. I can't imagine what's wrong with you. Where's your valet?"

"I only brought my tiger, Timmy," George muttered, trying to hide his disappointment and get control of himself. "He's seeing to the horses."

Felicia studied him, puzzled. "I don't understand you, Georgie. How can you possibly come to a party like this without a valet? Who will dress you?"

"Timmy will do," George retorted as he started up the stairs. "We're both quite capable of doing up buttons."

But, as it turned out, Timmy did not do at all. The lad was wonderful with horses, but he had no experience with dressing a gentleman. He botched the ironing of George's neckcloth, dropped a shirt-stud and spent long minutes searching for it, and clumsily tore the rosette from one of George's evening slippers. By the time this last disaster was discovered, it was so late that George feared everyone would have gone in to dinner without him. Hastily, he ripped the rosette from the other shoe and ran down the stairs toward the drawing room.

As he approached the doorway, the sound of laughing voices assured him that the guests had not yet gone in to dine. He paused in the doorway to get his breath and study the assemblage. They made a festive-looking group, the men standing about with their preprandial drinks in hand, their black evening coats making a dramatic background for the colorful, shimmering evening dresses of the ladies seated among them. George remembered that Felicia had said there would be ten at table, but he could see only seven in the room. He stood looking at them for a moment. One of them was bound to be she—his Venus. From his vantage point, he could see four ladies: a matronly woman standing with his brother-in-law, Leyton; his sister Felicia chatting with someone seated in an armchair and hidden by its wings; and two young ladies perched on a sofa, one of whom he recognized as the talkative Beatrice Rossiter. But the other, a decidedly pretty creature, was unknown to him. *Could she be*—? he wondered, his pulse beginning to race.

At that moment his brother-in-law noticed him in the doorway and instantly approached. Montague, Lord Leyton, was a string bean of a fellow with a keen mind and a kind heart. George was quite fond of him. "There you are, Georgie!" Leyton greeted eagerly and, clasping him affectionately by his shoulders, added in a whisper, "Thank goodness you're here. The Thomsett brothers haven't yet arrived, and we've no other bachelor on the premises but you to entertain three single females!" Then he drew his brother-in-law into the room, saying loudly, "Come, let me make you known to everyone. I say, Sylvia," he cried to the matronly woman, "this is Felicia's brother. George, this is Lady Sylvia Stoneham."

"I've been so looking forward to meeting you, Lord Chadleigh," the lady chirped in a birdlike voice quite unsuited to her voluminous frame. "Felicia sings your praises quite constantly."

"Something she never does to my face," George quipped as he bowed over her hand.

Felicia looked up at those words, said something to the person in the wing chair, and approached. "Don't mind him, Lady Sylvia," she said with a laugh. "He knows very well that he's my favorite brother."

"Of course, since he's your *only* brother," Leyton put in. "But never mind the nonsense, and let me introduce George to Lord Stoneham."

Lord Stoneham, large-bellied and pompously slow, came up beside his wife. "Howdedo, Chadleigh." He lifted the monocle that hung on a cord round his neck and peered at George through it. "Yes, I thought so. You're George Frobisher. You won't remember, but I played against you in a cricket match at school. I played for Queens, and you for Trinity. You were just a freshman, do you remember?"

"Yes, of course," George lied. "How good to see you again."

"This is no time to speak of sports and games," Felicia said decidedly, taking George's arm. "He must meet the others."

Relieved and thankful to be spared more school reminiscences, George let his sister lead him to the sofa. He was introduced to Miss Beatrice Rossiter first. *Ah, the talkative one that Felicia said was shy,* he reminded himself. She held out her hand to him, her full cheeks turning red and her light blue eyes not quite meeting his. *Yes,* he thought, *she is indeed shy.* It was a quality he had no recollection of, but in order to move on to the next introduction, he quickly declared, "I remember you very well indeed." Then, with an eagerness he feared was more appropriate to a seventeen-year-old innocent than a twenty-seven-year-old sophisticate, he turned toward the other young lady on the sofa. "And you are—?" he asked, his eyes raking over her burnished coppery curls, her soft eyes, full lips, and her full-bosomed form that looked utterly enticing under a mauve peau-de-soie gown. Though her curves were more ample than his memories of his Venus, he excused her in his mind. *Ten years,* he thought in generous forgiveness, *might have added a bit of fullness to those delicious curves I remember.* He was quite willing to be pleased.

Felicia took due note of the gleam in her brother's eyes. "Georgie," she said with a triumphant smile, "this is Miss Elaine Whitmore."

Whitmore? Not Henshaw? George was too well trained in social etiquette to let his disappointment show. "Delighted to meet you, Miss Whitmore," he said, lifting her hand to his lips.

Leyton came up behind him at that moment. "And we mustn't forget to make you known to Miss Henshaw," he declared, pointing toward the fireplace and the winged chair.

George felt his spirits lift again. *At last!* he thought, his blood bubbling up again in his veins. "Yes, Miss Henshaw by all means!"

They came up behind the chair. "George, may I present our dear friend, Miss Olivia Henshaw. Livy, turn round and say a how-de-do to my brother-in-law, George."

"Miss Henshaw," George said, an eager smile lighting his face. "I've long been looking forward—"

She turned and looked up at him. At the meeting of their eyes, the world seemed to freeze. The words he was about to say caught in his throat. It was as if he'd been boxing with a weakling who'd suddenly turned and dealt him a smashing blow to his stomach. He almost reeled. Was *this* his Venus? It couldn't be true! She was so far from what he'd imagined that he was stunned. Of course, he'd never really seen her face, but *this* face— the eyes starkly dark, the skin pallid, the cheeks hollow, and the lips thin and pursed as if in utter disapproval of all those eyes looked upon—did not seem to belong to the body he remembered. Even the body that he now saw could not be the same. The spare form he could discern under the dark blue muslin dress bore no resemblance to the luscious curves he so clearly remembered. From the top of her head, where her dull brown hair was pinned in a severe bun, to the hem of her governess-like dress, she was in no way a Venus.

His dream, his Venus, his Olivia Henshaw, was but *a dried-up spinster!*

Sophisticated though he was, he was incapable of hiding his shock. He could feel his jaw drop, and he knew his eyes must reveal something of his distress. Miss Henshaw did not misread his expression. She stared at him in cool surprise. "I seem to have disappointed you, Lord Chadleigh," she said.

"Oh, no," George said quickly, feeling his neck reddening. "No, indeed."

"Then why do you look so . . . so crestfallen?"

Damn the woman, he thought in despair. *On top of everything else, she's blunt to a fault.* "Well, I . . . you see, er . . ." he mumbled.

"Yes?" she asked, eyeing him askance.

He had to take himself in hand. "Neither disappointed nor crestfallen, ma'am," he said, forcing a smile. "Only surprised. I . . . er . . . expected someone else."

"*Another* Olivia Henshaw?" Her voice was heavy with sarcasm.

"Well, I . . . I . . ."

"Good God, Georgie," Leyton muttered in his ear, "what's wrong with you?"

But George was saved further embarrassment by the butler's announcement that dinner was served.

"Let me take you in, Livy," Leyton said, gently elbowing the stunned George aside and offering the lady his arm.

Miss Henshaw rose and took it. As they passed the still-stricken George, Miss Henshaw did not look at him. Leyton urged her to go on ahead for a moment and, leaning close to George's ear, hissed, "Don't stand there like a clunch, man. Pull yourself together and escort Miss Whitmore in. She's more your style, eh?"

George gave himself a shake and did as he was bid. The hosts and their guests took their seats at the table, and dinner commenced with what seemed like perfectly

ordinary good spirits. But to George, the atmosphere
seemed unreal. Nightmarish. He hardly heard what was
being said to him, though he managed to answer the
questions being thrown at him by the lovely Miss Whitmore on his left and to obey the demands for attention
of the overbearing Lady Sophy on his right. Although
Miss Henshaw was seated on the other side of the table,
as far from him as it was possible to be, he could not
keep himself from looking over at her every few moments. It was a strange compulsion, not unlike the tendency to pick at a painful scab one is ordered not to
touch. At one point Felicia remarked aloud that her
brother seemed unusually quiet, but Lady Sophy patted
his arm and declared she liked the quiet sort. Miss
Whitmore, too, seemed content enough with his monosyllabic replies to her remarks. He himself thought he
did quite well under the circumstances. After all, he was
a man in mourning. A long-cherished dream had just
died.

Four

*F*elicia was not happy. Her house party was not proceeding in the lively way she'd hoped. It seemed as if a fog of boredom had settled in over the entire assemblage. Here it was only ten o'clock in the evening, and everyone already looked sleepy. Poor Beatrice was singing "My Mother Bids Me Bind My Hair" with such quavering nervousness that it caused the listeners to feel discomfort at first and boredom at last. Lady Sophy was nodding, Georgie was staring straight ahead in the most unusual abstraction, and her own dear Leyton was stifling a yawn.

The song was entering its third chorus when the butler, Kelby, tiptoed in and whispered to Felicia that the Thomsetts had arrived. *Thank goodness,* she thought, leaping to her feet. *Perhaps a pair of new arrivals will enliven us.*

Her abrupt movement caused Beatrice to stop right in the middle of a phrase. "Sorry," Felicia murmured with a helpless shrug. "Do go on, Beatrice dear." And with the stealthiest of steps, she followed Kelby out of the room.

In the foyer Kelby was helping the newly arrived gentlemen with their coats. Felicia paused a moment to study them. The new arrivals were not quite as prepossessing as her husband had led her to expect. One was a large man with powerful shoulders and a broad midsection, weighing a good three stone more than his undersized, pallid brother. But appearances were often deceiving, she warned herself. With a sprinkling of wit or some charm of address they might do very well. Swallowing her disappointment, she put on a smile and greeted them. "I'm sorry Leyton is not with me," she apologized, "but we could not both desert our guests."

"Of course not, your ladyship," the tall Thomsett said. "Our fault entirely for arriving so late. May I introduce myself? I'm Sir Horace Thomsett, and this is my brother Algernon."

"I'm so glad to meet you at last," Felicia said, offering her hand to both. "Leyton has sung your praises so often."

Horace turned her aside, and in a hushed voice explained that his brother, Algernon, had taken ill on the road. "It was an attack of pernicious dyspepsia," he murmured, "so severe that we felt it necessary to stop at an inn until the symptoms abated."

But his brother heard every word. "You needn't whisper," he said querulously, "and you needn't make so much of a simple stomach upset caused by the rocking of the coach. I assure you, Lady Felicia, that I'm much better now."

"Are you sure?" Felicia asked, turning to him. "Would you wish me to send for the doctor? Our Dr. Simmons is very good."

"No, I think a good night's sleep is all Algy needs," Horace declared firmly.

"Really, Horace," his brother whined, "I wish you wouldn't always speak for me. But I suppose going to sleep would be wise."

"Then you must go to bed at once," Felicia said, and with a nod of her head, summoned the butler to show him the way.

Horace watched as the smaller brother followed Kelby up the stairs. "He'll be a new man in the morning, you'll see," he assured Felicia.

"Do you suppose," Felicia asked worriedly, "that he might wish a bit of supper brought up to his room?"

"No, I'm certain he won't, although I myself must admit to being hungry."

Felicia, resigning herself to the fact that these new arrivals would be no help at all in animating the party, nodded and led him to the morning room, where she offered him an aperitif while the remnants of the dinner were hastily reheated and brought to him. By the time he'd satisfied his hunger, the other guests had gone up to bed. "You'll meet the others in the morning," Felicia said with an apologetic smile as she bid him good night. But, she realized belatedly, with the men going off for some shooting, and the ladies probably staying abed for half the morning, there would not be an opportunity for proper introductions until teatime.

Later that night, Felicia tapped at her brother's door. George was already half asleep. Bleary-eyed, barefoot, and in his nightshirt, he only partially opened the door. "You woke me," he muttered reproachfully. Then, peering at her in the dim light of the candle she carried, he saw that she, too, was barefoot, although she was otherwise fully covered by a purple peignoir made voluminous by row upon row of lacy flounces. He couldn't help laughing. "You look like a bunch of grapes," he said.

She glared at him. "Thank you for the compliment. But never mind. May I come in?"

"At this late hour?"

"Oh, pooh, it's not even eleven." She brushed past him, placed her candle on his night table, and perched on his bed. "I want to talk to you."

Capitulating, he closed the door and followed her. "Talk to me about what?"

"About what you think about her," Felicia prodded eagerly.

"What is there to think about?" He threw himself upon a chair and replied grumpily, "She's just as you said—too old for me."

Felicia blinked in surprise. "Too old? What nonsense! She's barely twenty!"

"Barely twenty? She looks forty to the day!" He eyed

his sister suspiciously. "Didn't you tell me she's two years your senior?"

"I never said such a ridiculous thing! She's younger than Beatrice, and Beatrice is a good eight years younger than I. Looks forty, indeed! Lady Sophy is forty, perhaps, but the only one under this roof who's close to my age is—" She gasped as an idea suddenly burst upon her. "Goodness me, Georgie, are you speaking of *Livy*?"

"Who else would I be speaking of?"

"You *are* a clunch! I told you quite plainly I didn't invite you for Livy. It's Elaine I've invited you to meet."

George's jaw dropped. "Have you been questioning me about *Miss Whitmore*?"

"Of course!"

"Oh!" He dropped his eyes from her face, feeling very foolish indeed.

Felicia studied him with knitted brow. "What made you think I wanted to speak to you of Livy? Does she interest you somehow?"

"No, of course not. This is a silly conversation. Go away, Felicia, and let me get to sleep."

"She doesn't at all look forty."

"Very well, she doesn't. I shouldn't have said it. You know I'm a complete looby about such things."

"Yes, you are." Felicia, her brow still furrowed, got up and started toward the door. "So you have nothing to say about Elaine?"

"What is it you wish me to say?"

Felicia wheeled about in annoyance. "That she's lovely. That you're taken with her. That she's just the sort you'd like to wed."

George snorted. Handing her the candle, he turned her toward the door. "She's a very pleasing young woman. And that, sister dear, is all you'll get from me." And, firmly propelling her out to the corridor, he wished her a very final "Good night."

Five

*B*ack in her room, Felicia climbed into bed beside her husband. Leyton sat up and studied her, trying to judge the success of her mission without prodding. He saw at once that it had not gone well. "Well, what did he say?" he asked at last.

"He said she's pleasant."

"That's not very promising," Leyton said.

"No, it's not. He doesn't show any interest in Elaine at all."

"Well, I warned you. He's never shown any interest in shallow females like Elaine, though he's certainly had dozens like her thrown at him. I told you he wouldn't be different this time."

"But she's so very beautiful. I'd hoped—"

"It's a very superficial beauty, if you ask me," Leyton muttered.

"Evidently Georgie thinks so, too," Felicia sighed, discouraged. She leaned back against the pillows and turned a pair of puzzled eyes to her husband's face. "Do you want to hear something quizzy, dearest? I think he's interested in *Livy!*"

Leyton gave a scornful snort. "That's ridiculous. He was positively rude to her when I introduced them."

"Rude? *Georgie?*" She couldn't believe her ears. "In what way? Georgie would never be rude to a lady! What did he say that you thought was rude?"

"It wasn't quite what he said. It was how he looked.

As if . . . as if . . . Oh, I don't know." He scratched his head in a gesture of helplessness. "I can't explain. It's only a feeling. Let's forget it and go to sleep."

But Felicia couldn't drop the subject. "I don't understand it. There's something strange about all this. When I asked him about Elaine, before I actually mentioned her name, he immediately assumed I was speaking of Livy. As if Elaine had not made the slightest impression on him! How is it possible that Livy, who is not breathtaking even when she's in looks—and these days she's certainly not at all at her best—can have impressed my flirtatious brother more than the spectacular Elaine?"

"Elaine is a silly flibbertigibbet," Leyton muttered, snuggling into his pillow. "Livy is worth ten of her."

"Yes, I know that, but she's not in Georgie's style. Besides, she's too old for him."

"Right. We've pinned our hopes for Livy on Horace, haven't we?"

"*You* have." Felicia heaved a heavy sigh. "I no longer have hopes in that direction."

"No?" He turned round and raised himself on his elbow. "Why not?"

"Really, my love, your friends the Thomsetts are not at all what I expected. I don't believe Livy will take to Horace at all."

"How can you say so? Horace is the best of fellows, I assure you."

"Perhaps he is, among the fellows you associate with, but I don't think *my* friends will find him so."

"Come now, my love," Leyton objected, "you barely know him."

"I know enough."

"Do you indeed?" Leyton, irked by her attitude, pulled himself up to a sitting position again. "What makes you believe your judgment is superior to mine, when I've known him for five years and you've known him for five minutes?"

"Because, my dear, women often notice things that men miss altogether."

"You don't say! And what exactly did you discover in five minutes that I've missed all these years?"

"I discovered that his own brother finds him overbearing."

"Humph!" Leyton snorted. "Discovered by feminine intuition, no doubt. I don't suppose you can give me any logical evidence for that supposition, can you?"

"I certainly can. For one thing, your friend Horace gave all the orders. And, for another, little Algy complained that Horace never let him answer for himself."

"That's just not—" Leyton stopped himself in midsentence. Something in what his wife had said rang true. He thought the matter over for a moment. "Perhaps you're in the right of it," he admitted finally. "Horace does have the habit of speaking for Algy sometimes."

Having won her point, Felicia refrained from gloating. "Well, never mind," she said, leaning over and bestowing a kiss on Leyton's brow. "This party will probably be a disaster, but we shall make the best of it." She blew out the candle and slipped down under the counterpane. "Thank goodness my invitation was only for the weekend."

"Yes," her husband agreed, putting a comforting arm about her shoulders, "it's fortunate you didn't invite them for a sennight!"

"That would *certainly* have been a disaster." She nestled into his embrace and sighed. "I hoped that at least one romance might blossom as a result of this gathering."

"Don't give up hope, my love. Perhaps Elaine will take to Horace."

"I don't think so. She seems already to have set her sights on Georgie, worse luck."

"I wouldn't despair, if I were you," Leyton murmured, his lips against her hair. "You may yet be surprised. Beatrice may set her sights on Horace, or Livy may astound us all and take to Algy."

"I doubt it," Felicia said mournfully. "Besides, I was thinking of Algy for Beatrice. Dash it all, if Georgie has no interest in Elaine, my entire plan for the weekend is bound to fail."

Leyton gave up. "Well, good night, my dear," he murmured.

His wife lifted her head. "Good night?" she cried. "Is that all you have to say?"

"What else can I say? Except that it's quite plain to me that neither you nor I has any talent for matchmaking." With that, he pulled her back into his embrace and asked plaintively, "Now may we please go to sleep?"

Six

*B*ack in London, Bernard woke on Friday morning with a feeling of alarm without knowing why. Then he remembered. George was gone! He'd left yesterday for Yorkshire. His best friend had deserted him just when he most needed support.

Of course, there was not yet any cause for alarm. The Renwood ball was still five days away, and George had given his word to return in time. But anything might happen to keep him from fulfilling his promise. There were all sorts of possibilities for delay. It was winter. The weather might make travel difficult. A snowstorm could make the roads impassable. An accident to the carriage could occur in an unpopulated place. An unexpected illness could strike. Or George could become infatuated with his mysterious lady and forget his promise.

Feeling decidedly depressed, he heaved himself up and, supporting himself by the bedpost, rang for his man. "After all," he muttered aloud, "he did say she was very lovely. It's quite possible that he could become besotted."

"Who's besotted?" came a voice from the doorway. It was Pratkin, his valet since his college days. After all the years of service, there was little formality between master and man.

"No one," Bernard said shortly. "I was only thinking out loud."

"About Lord Frobisher, I have no doubt," the valet

said, handing Bernard his crutches. "He said he'd be back, and he will. His lordship is not the type to go back on his word."

Bernard eyed his man for a moment and then nodded. Pratkin's words were reassuring. They made him remember that George was the sort who'd overcome every obstacle to keep his word. "Yes, you're right," he admitted at last. "He wouldn't forget a promise. Not George."

However, he remained uneasy. After all, the best laid plans, as the Scottish poet Robert Burns warned, often go awry.

Later, to cheer himself, he decided to take luncheon at Brooks' club. He could have chosen White's or Boodle's, where he was just as well known, but the fellows at Brooks' were more Whiggish than Tory and thus more congenial to him. He set off in his carriage in passably good spirits, but the chill of the air changed his mood again. It was stingingly cold and smelled of snow. If it did snow, then all the dread possibilities he'd imagined earlier could come to pass. "Drat!" he cursed aloud. "Must we have a storm at just this time?"

Pratkin, perched up on the box beside the coachman, heard him. "There won't be any storm," he said as he helped Bernard down from the carriage in front of Brooks'.

"Much you know about predicting weather," Bernard snapped, but he added more kindly, "Don't wait out here in the cold. Just come back for me at three."

The coach drove off. Bernard swung himself about on his crutches with the expertise of ten years' experience, and he started toward the club's entrance in firm control of his movements. At that moment, however, a strong gust of wind swept down St. James's Street, dislodging his tall beaver hat from his head and sending it rolling along the pavement. "Damnation," he swore as he made an attempt to follow it. After three awkward heaves on his crutches, however, he knew it was hopeless. The hat was already dozens of yards beyond his reach.

Suddenly a seedy-looking fellow appeared from round

the corner and made a dive for the beaver. He caught it
with hands covered by shabby, fingerless gloves. The fellow eyed the tall hat with admiration and brushed the
dust from its brim with loving care.

"Oh, I say, my good man, I do thank you!" Bernard
shouted gratefully.

The fellow looked over at the crippled Bernard and
grinned. "Ye'r welcome, sir, I'm sure," he shouted back.
Then, clapping the hat on his own head, he laughed
heartily, thumbed his nose at Bernard, and took off in
the opposite direction, rounding the corner at Pall Mall
and disappearing from sight.

Bernard's lips tightened in helpless frustration. *How,*
he wondered, *can I be such a damned fool?* Ordinarily,
he was quite comfortable with his handicap, having become accustomed to dealing with the difficulties it pre-
sented, but on occasions like this one, the awareness of
his limitations cut him to the quick. Waves of frustration
and self-disgust washed over him. He stood trembling in
fury until an inner voice reminded him that the poor
wretch of a hat-robber had a great deal more need for
a warm hat than he had.

Thus consoled, he heaved a sigh of acceptance and
turned back toward the club's doorway. But with a hand
on the doorknob, he hesitated again. If he made an appearance without a hat, there would surely be questions.
He'd feel even more the fool than he already did if he
had to explain . . .

Then he remembered that Lock's, the hat shop, was
just down St. James's, only a short distance from where
he stood. Since he could get there without too much
effort and buy himself a new beaver, he promptly set off
in that direction.

He'd gone but a few steps and was passing Berry
Brothers, a fashionable shop for wines and imported
spices, when a pair of females emerged from the doorway
and started across the pavement toward a waiting carriage. Bernard took only the slightest notice of them, but
they noticed him. "Sir Bernard!" cried one of them.

He turned his head and, to his horror, recognized Lady Renwood and her daughter. He felt himself go pale. "Lady Renwood! M-M-Miss Harriet!" he stammered, turning about awkwardly and putting his hand up to lift the hat that wasn't there. "Er . . . ah . . . good d-d-day."

"What a pleasant surprise to run into you this way," her ladyship gushed. "But where is your hat?"

Now he felt himself flush. "It blew away, I'm afraid. I'm just on my way to purchase another."

"What a shame!" the younger lady exclaimed, putting a hand on his arm in a gesture of sincere sympathy.

The little gesture touched him. He looked down at the girl, his heart clenching in his chest. She was quite lovely, her eyes laughing up at him, and the reddish curls of her hair peeping out from the brim of her feathered bonnet. The warmth of her expression was enough to embolden him. He smiled shyly down at her. "I fear I make quite an unpresentable appearance."

"Well, your hair's a bit windblown," Harriet said, grinning back at him, "but it makes you look—how shall I say?—sort of Byronic. Rather dashing, wouldn't you say, Mama?"

"Byronic is just the word." Lady Renwood nodded, smiling fondly.

Bernard, unable to picture the vibrant Lord Byron on crutches, couldn't help snorting. "Oh, yes, Byronic indeed."

But the young lady would not be contradicted. "Since you can't see yourself, and we can, you must take our word for how dashing you look."

Before Bernard could reply, Lady Renwood took a step forward and poked his chest with an indignant finger. "You naughty boy," she scolded, "are you aware that you haven't yet sent your reply to our invitation? You are coming to my ball on Wednesday, aren't you?"

Bernard stiffened. "I hope to, your ladyship, but, you see, Lord Frobisher has gone north, and I'm not sure he'll return on time."

Harriet stared at him, her smile fading. "What has Lord Frobisher to do with it?"

"I rely on him, you see."

"I'm afraid," the girl replied, stiffening, "that I *don't* see."

Her mother poked her with an elbow. "Of course we see! It is perfectly reasonable, in your circumstances, to want someone with you. We must hope that Lord Frobisher returns on time." With a glance at her daughter, as if advising her that the conversation had gone on long enough, she started toward her carriage. "Come, Harriet, we mustn't keep Sir Bernard standing about in the cold."

Her ladyship gave him a good-bye nod, but as the footman was about to hand her up into the carriage, she turned again to Bernard. "We shall put you on the guest list," she said kindly, "but if you don't come, we shall certainly understand."

Bernard forced a smile. "Thank you, your ladyship."

Harriet, who'd slowly followed her mother, suddenly shook off the footman's arm and marched back to where Bernard stood leaning on his crutches watching her. She stood before him, arms akimbo and hands on hips. "Mama may understand," she said in a strangely ominous tone, "but I won't." With that, she stomped back to the coach, sloughed off the offer of help from the footman, jumped in, and pulled the carriage door closed with a slam.

Bernard stared after them as the carriage rumbled off. *What did she mean by that?* he asked himself. Did she mean that she didn't see why he needed George's company? Or did she mean she'd be unforgiving if he didn't make an appearance—that, in other words, she *wanted* him to come? If she was suggesting that she wished for his company, that would be very good news. But she was angry when she said it. Could she be angry at him and wish for his company at the same time?

He sighed in utter confusion. Harriet's brief remark had put him decidedly out of countenance. Without

George to explain the subtleties of the feminine mind to him, he would worry himself over those few words for the remaining five days. *Oh, blast!* he cursed inwardly, *blast Harriet, blast her mother, and blast the whole female sex!*

Seven

*I*n Yorkshire, shortly after dawn on Friday morning, three men gathered for the shooting expedition— Leyton, Lord Stoneham, and George. But just as Kelby appeared with a tray of hot toddies to warm the hunters before they set off, Horace Thomsett clamored down the stairs. "Oh, good!" he chortled. "You haven't left yet!"

Leyton was surprised. "Well, well, Horace, old fellow, I'm glad to see you," he greeted. "After your late arrival yesterday, I didn't expect you up so early."

"Getting up wasn't a hardship for me," Horace said with hearty enthusiasm. "Algy ain't up to it, but I've been looking forward to a good shoot since the day you sent me the invitation."

The other men heartily agreed. A good shoot was just what they wanted, and after hasty introductions and equally hasty downing of their drinks, they shouldered their rifles and started off. They were all in high good humor, in spite of the overcast sky and a cold wind. But they'd no sooner flushed out their first flock of grouse when an icy rain began to fall. It continued to fall steadily throughout the morning, the downpour squelching their spirits and their marksmanship. By the time they gave up and turned back toward home, they had gained only a cold soaking to their hunting jackets and two dead birds. It was a glum and sodden group that tramped back to the Abbey.

As soon as they'd changed into dry clothes, they one

by one made their way downstairs to the East Salon where the ladies were gathered. The sight before them of the enticing ladies, who'd spread themselves about the room in various poses of ennui, and the smell of hot food emanating from a large buffet table set before the windows were enough to restore their good spirits. In short order they were sipping Felicia's famous hot drink called Lambs' Wool (a concoction of hot cider, home brew, and wine) and loading their plates with cheese biscuits, honeyed ham slices, coddled eggs, cabbage flowers with Parmesan, and sugared buns.

Thus warmed and provisioned, they mingled with the ladies, answering questions about their morning's activity by transforming their misadventures into feats of comic or heroic proportions. Horace regaled Beatrice and Elaine with a boastful account of how he managed to shoot one of the two birds they'd snared, while George set his sister and Lady Stoneham into peals of laughter by demonstrating how one tries to take aim on a high-flying bird while sleet is pelting down on the eyelids.

Algy, who'd come down before the hunters returned, had managed to insinuate himself beside Beatrice. His altercation with his brother the night before had stiffened his backbone, and he was determined to come out from behind his brother's shadow and assert himself. "You, Miss Rossiter," he declared boldly, "are the prettiest creature in this room."

The shy little lady, who usually tried to hide that shyness by babbling about anything that came to her head, was so flustered by this astounding compliment that she was stricken dumb. Thus Algy was able to hold forth, uninterrupted, on his favorite topics—the problems of London's sanitation and the ridiculousness of tying one's neckcloth in complicated folds. With Beatrice's wide eyes fixed on him attentively, he glowed with pride.

When the hunters returned, Algy called his brother aside. "I think I've made a mark on that young lady over there," he whispered urgently, "so I warn you, if you wish to avoid a frightful *contretemps,* don't dare interfere with me!"

Horace only shrugged. He was not interested in Beatrice. He'd already intended to make Elaine the object of his attentions, and he promptly and purposefully crossed the room to her and sat down beside her. Elaine, however, had other plans: she rose from her chair and crossed the room to where George was holding forth. The rapt manner with which she listened to his account of the shooting adventure made it plain to Horace that he had no chance with her. He therefore turned to Olivia, who was sitting a little apart from the others. Pulling up an ottoman beside her chair, he perched upon it and began again to describe to her his amazing prowess in shooting a grouse against such terrible odds.

George, having relinquished the floor to his brother-in-law, stepped back out of the circle and, sipping his drink, studied the people in the room. Again, as on the night before, he found his eyes drawn toward Olivia Henshaw. He couldn't help noticing that though she kept her eyes on Horace's face, she shifted in her chair and twice tried to excuse herself. But Horace seemed to be engaged in a long-winded monologue that gave her no opportunity to do so. For no reason that he could account for, George decided to go to her aid. He put his glass down on the sideboard and crossed the room to her. "I beg pardon, Thomsett," he cut into the monologue, "but my sister is asking for you."

"Oh, is she?" The big fellow pulled himself to his feet and bowed to Olivia. "Excuse me, Miss Henshaw. I shall be back directly." And after awkwardly backing up a few steps, he bowed again, turned, and hurried away.

George stood looking down at her. "Did you want something, Miss Henshaw? I had the impression you were trying to rise."

"Had you, indeed?" She gazed up at him shrewdly. "Then your sister didn't really ask for Mr. Thomsett, did she?"

"No." George threw her a small, conspiratorial smile. "I thought you might need rescuing."

She did not return the smile. "That was good of you, my lord," she said coolly, "but I was not in need of rescuing. I'm quite capable of taking care of myself."

George was taken aback. "I assure you, ma'am, that I meant no disrespect."

"I'm sure you didn't. It is disrespectful nonetheless to assume that someone is helpless when she isn't at all."

"You're quite right, of course," he said, but he seethed inside. He'd tried to do a good deed, and she was turning the kindly act into an insult. But he could see that it would do no good to argue the point. He would let it pass. "I do apologize," he said.

She nodded and looked away. Her manner made it clear that she was dismissing him. This infuriated him even more. Who did this spindly old maid think she was to dismiss him in that high-handed way, the Queen of the Realm?

He stood his ground. "May I sit down?" he asked.

"Here?" She seemed truly surprised.

"Yes, of course here. You didn't think I was asking your permission to sit across the room, did you?"

"Well, I . . . I . . ." She was obviously flustered. "I . . . didn't think you'd . . ."

"You didn't think I'd what?"

"I didn't think you'd wish for my . . ." Her eyes flitted up to his and down again. "Never mind."

"Then may I sit down?" he persisted.

She looked over her shoulder as if hoping for a rescuer. "I think Mr. Thomsett is starting back," she said in hurried refusal.

His eyebrows rose in mock offense. "Don't tell me you want to save this seat for *him*! Are you truly interested in hearing again how, despite the sleet, he managed to direct his bullet right into the bird's eyeball?"

She winced at the words, but a little laugh bubbled up from her chest despite her effort to stifle it. "Oh, sit down, sit down!" she said helplessly. "You, Lord Chadleigh, have a decided streak of—if I may be blunt—of assertiveness in you."

He dropped down on the ottoman. "Assertiveness? That, ma'am, is not being blunt. It's being tactful. I think you really mean impudence."

"That *is* being blunt. But yes, that's just what I mean."

"And you're quite right to recognize it. It's a quality I encourage in myself."

"Yes, you would," she retorted in dry disapproval.

He cocked his head at her. "By the tone of that remark, ma'am, I conclude that you've made a quick assessment of my whole character. A negative one."

"Well, impudence can scarcely be considered a positive characteristic, can it?"

"It certainly can," he insisted, "if one is disposed to be positive."

"How, my lord, can impudence be looked at as a good?"

"Think about it, ma'am." He leaned toward her, speaking with earnest persuasiveness. "To be impudent, one must have courage, right?"

"The courage to be rude, perhaps," she said, dismissing his point with a wave.

"But courage, nevertheless, to be able to speak out," he persisted, smiling at her. "And if one is talented at being impudent, honesty is essential. To that must be added a sense of humor—wit, if you will. Wit can give impudence a veneer of charm."

"That is frivolous nonsense, my lord," she said, refusing to smile back. "Pure self-justification, nothing more. Impudence is neither courage nor honesty nor wit. It is simply rudeness, defiance, disrespect, and, at its worst, unkindness."

His expression darkened, the earlier fury he'd felt toward her rising up in him again. "And in your quick assessment of my character is that how you see me— rude and unkind?" He threw her an ironic sneer. "You, ma'am, if I may be blunt, have a decided streak of . . . of the judgmental in you."

"Judgmental?" She did not miss the irony in his expression. "That, my lord, is not being blunt. It is being tactful. I think you really mean contemptuous."

"That *is* being blunt." He studied her for a long moment. Never before had he believed that anyone could hold him in contempt. "It seems," he said at last, "that you have little liking for me."

Her eyes dropped from his face. "It seems we have little liking for each other."

George heard those words with a sudden feeling that they might not be as true for him as they were for her. But there was no time now to analyze the feeling. After what she'd just said, he could not remain sitting there. "Then I suppose I'd best turn this seat back to Mr. Thomsett," he muttered, rising. "He's standing just behind you, waiting for his opportunity."

He walked swiftly away, but when he'd crossed the room he found himself looking back at her. She was apparently listening to Horace, but her eyes looked absent. Her face was motionless, expressionless. But he had to admit the intelligence of her eyes and her high forehead, the sculptured spareness of her cheekbones, the proud chin, and slender neck all combined to give her a look of admirable dignity. *Strange,* he thought, *how different she appears now from the way she looked only last night.* She was no Venus, certainly, but she was not a spindly old maid either.

Eight

As her abigail arranged a row of small curls along the sides of her face, Felicia smiled at her own reflection in the dressing-table mirror. "Oh, Katie, that's perfect—just as I wanted it," she exclaimed.

"Thank ye, ma'am," the maid said, dousing the coals that had heated the curling iron. "Shall ye be wearin' the dark green crepe tonight?"

"No. The amber Florentine, I think." She rose from the dressing table and whirled round in pleasure, spinning easily on the soles of her new dancing slippers. "I want to look as cheerful as I feel."

Everything pleased her this evening—her hair, her new slippers, and the prospect of appearing before her guests in a gown of glowing yellow. She was at last beginning to enjoy the party she'd so carefully arranged. In spite of the sleet that had spoiled their morning, her guests had begun to warm to each other. The late breakfast had produced some animated moments, the afternoon games (they'd played penny loo and had haggled like children) had engendered much laughter, and she was certain that the evening ahead, unlike the night before, would be a lively affair. The cook had promised to prepare his outstanding *poulaille filets à la marechale,* which was sure to please the most discriminating palate, and his Turkish Mosque Ruin would end the meal with oohs and aahs. The glow was bound to last throughout the evening, even if Beatrice should decide to sing again.

Just as the thought of Beatrice crossed Felicia's mind, the girl herself appeared at the dressing-room door. "May I speak to you, Felicia?" she whispered, glancing nervously at the abigail.

"Of course, Beatrice, my dear," Felicia assured her, while throwing Katie a meaningful glance. "Do come in."

The abigail promptly slipped out of the room, tactfully closing the door behind her. Felicia motioned Beatrice to the chaise—the room's only furnishing other than the dressing table and its little upholstered bench. Felicia herself perched on the bench and looked over at her visitor curiously. "Is something troubling you?" she asked kindly.

Beatrice lowered her light eyes to the hands clenched in her lap. "No, not exactly. I'm having a perfectly lovely time, really I am. I know I didn't sing very well last night, but you know how addled I get when I have to perform before strangers, and then, right in the middle of the song, I realized that I'd chosen the wrong selection, it should have been something livelier, something more—"

Felicia cut her off. "Beatrice, you're chattering. And you know that you only start chattering when you get nervous. But surely you needn't be nervous with me." She leaned over and took her visitor's hands in hers. "Tell me what's troubling you. Whatever it is, I shall understand."

"Well, I . . . I—"

"Do speak up, dearest. What is it?" Felicia urged. "It can't be last night's singing. Your voice was lovely and the song just right."

"No, it's not the singing. It's—" She looked up at Felicia and took a deep breath. "It's Algy. I think he's"—a flush of color rose up in her full cheeks—"he's taken with me."

Felicia suppressed the urge to laugh. "Is he? I'm not at all surprised. And are you taken with him, too?"

Beatrice dropped her eyes again. "Perhaps. But I . . . I know so little about him. He's a bit shy, you see."

"Is he really?" Felicia murmured. "I'd not have guessed—"

Beatrice suddenly turned an intent gaze on her friend's face. "What do you think of him, Felicia? Tell me the truth. Do you like him?"

Felicia hesitated. This is what she'd hoped would happen when she planned the party, but now her brief acquaintance with the Thomsett brothers had shaken her confidence. "Well, you know, I only just met him," she said carefully, "but Leyton and Horace were at Cambridge together, and he's quite fond of both brothers."

"Is he? Truly?" Beatrice seemed pleased, but her curiosity was evidently not yet satisfied. "You know, Felicia," she murmured, lowering her voice to a mere whisper, "Algy's the younger of the two . . ."

Felicia knew just what Beatrice was trying to ask. It was something every young woman had to know before embarking on a courtship. "Yes, he is the younger," she replied to the unasked question, "but he has an estate of his own. I'm of the impression that both men are well to pass. Algy, I believe, in addition to being well established in the funds, is part owner of his brother's bank."

Beatrice beamed. "Thank you, my dear," she said, jumping to her feet, "that's just what I wanted to know." She planted a kiss on Felicia's cheek and went to the door. But there she paused. "Oh, one thing more," she said, sounding nervous again. "You don't think he's too short for me, do you?"

This was too much for Felicia. She let out a peal of laughter. As a long-married woman, she knew that of all the things that can cause difficulties between a man and a woman, size was the least important. "As to his being short," she said, jumping up and urging the girl gently out the door, "I'm certain that he's as tall as I am, and you know, Beatrice, that I stand at least an inch over you."

A few moments later, as Katie was tying the strings of

her corset, Felicia realized that her cheerful mood had evaporated. She was troubled about her conversation with Beatrice. She hadn't meant to encourage the girl's feelings for Algy. After all, the fellow had shown himself to be rather milk-and-water toward his brother. Was he a mollycoddle? And if so, was that the sort of man she wished for her friend?

Before she could frame an answer in her mind, there was another tap at the door and Elaine burst in, carrying two gowns over her arm. Without preamble she held up the first for Felicia to see. "Which one?" she asked. "This, the blue silk? Or this, the lilac brocade?"

Felicia blinked. "I don't know. They both—"

Elaine held the lilac up to her neck and then substituted the blue. "There. The blue accents my eyes, but the lilac has more sweep, don't you think? Which one do you think he'd prefer?"

"He?" Felicia peered at her curiously. "Who?"

"Who do you think?" Elaine asked in disgust. "Your brother, of course."

"Oh." Felicia glanced uneasily at her abigail. "Katie, would you please go to fetch my . . . er . . ."

"You needn't send her off," Elaine said. "I shan't stay but a moment. Just tell me which is more likely to attract your Georgie."

"My 'Georgie' doesn't usually pay much attention to ladies' gowns," Felicia said.

"Nonsense. Of course he does. All men do. Let's be frank, Felicia. I believe your brother has shown a bit of interest in me, you see, but not enough. I intend to heighten that interest tonight. So tell me, my dear, which gown I should wear."

Felicia had been uncertain in her advice to Beatrice, but in this case she had no uncertainty; she did not want to offer Elaine any encouragement at all. She knew her brother well enough to recognize the difference between real attraction and mere politeness. George was behaving politely toward Elaine, that was all. "Both gowns are lovely," she said evasively.

"Hmm." Elaine held them both up and studied them. "The blue, I think. It's softer and has a deeper décolletage. The other may be too dignified." That decided, she nodded and started to the door. "Thank you, Felicia. I'm glad you made me decide for myself."

As soon as the door closed, Felicia sank down upon the chaise. *What have I done?* she asked herself. Because of her benighted plans, Beatrice might find herself betrothed to a mollycoddle, and Elaine was surely heading for a painful rejection. She couldn't help wondering if she'd done some harm to Livy, too. But no. Thank goodness Livy—her very best friend, and the last person on earth on whom she would wish to inflict pain—had too much sense to succumb to the attentions of the overbearing Horace.

However, as soon as she was dressed, she went down the hall to Livy's room to make sure her assessment of her friend's state of mind was correct. To her utter astonishment she found Livy sitting at her dressing table applying blacking to her eyelashes. "Livy!" she cried. "I thought you detested that sort of artificiality."

"I do." Livy grinned at her in the mirror and continued to apply the blacking. "But I must do something. I'm tired of looking like the spinster aunt you always invite to your parties out of pity."

"Oh, bosh," Felicia objected. "Spinster aunt, indeed. Who could possibly think such a thing?"

"Your brother, for one."

"Georgie? He wouldn't—!" But a sudden memory made her stop short. "Oh, dear. Leyton did say that Georgie was rude to you when you were introduced. Did he say something dreadful?"

"Not at all." Livy put down the blacking brush and turned to face her friend. "Your Georgie was polite to a fault. But something in his expression said quite plainly, *What on earth is this gaunt old maid doing here among these charming young women?*"

"Livy!" Felicia cried in offense. "How can you *think* such a thing? You're not being fair!"

"Am I not? Then why did Leyton tell you he was rude?"

"I don't know. But I know my brother. He would never be so unkind."

"Not aloud, perhaps. But one can't be blamed for one's thoughts. And don't deny it, Felicia, my sweet, but I *have* been looking like a gaunt old maid these days."

Felicia, not willing to accept so harsh a description, stepped back and studied her friend from top to toe. "As a matter of fact," she said sincerely, "you are quite in looks this evening. That dark red gown suits you."

"Does it? Are you sure?" She stood up and looked down at herself. "I almost didn't have the courage to wear it."

"It's perfect." Felicia threw her arms about her friend in a warm embrace. "It's so good to see you dressing up. You've been hiding yourself in dark shadows for so long!"

"I know. The cold Scottish mist seems to have settled in my innards. But your hospitality is warming me."

"I'm so glad." She dropped her arms from Livy's neck and grasped her hands. "I dearly wish for you to have a happy time while you're here. I know how hard it is for you to be happy at home."

Livy slipped her hands from Felicia's hold and turned away. "Yes," was all she said.

"By the way, Livy, dearest," Felicia said, as much to change a depressing subject as to reassure herself of her friend's enjoyment, "I noticed that Horace has been following you about. I hope you won't permit him to annoy you."

"Horace doesn't annoy me," Livy said. "He's really quite pleasant."

"Pleasant?" Felicia couldn't hide her surprise. "*Horace?*"

"I find him so."

Felicia gaped at her. Could Livy possibly have taken a fancy to such a fellow? The thought was preposterous.

Livy smiled at her friend's obvious dismay. "Don't worry about it, Felicia," she said soothingly. "I shan't marry the fellow. I find his attentions . . . er . . . convenient, that's all."

Felicia did not understand what her friend meant, but Livy's manner didn't seem to encourage further discussion. With a shrug, she let the matter drop. "Very well, my love. I'll leave you to your primping."

Livy returned to the dressing table as Felicia went to the door. "Felicia?" Livy called, staring into the mirror.

Felicia, her hand on the knob, looked back over her shoulder. "Yes, my love?"

"Should I take my hair down?"

Felicia grinned. "I've been wishing you would. With your hair down, no one could possibly take you for my spinster aunt."

Livy grinned back at Felicia's reflection in the glass. "Not even your brother?"

"Not even he."

But out in the corridor, Felicia's grin died. *What is going on?* she wondered. Was Livy dressing up for Horace or to take some sort of revenge on Georgie? The revelations of the past half hour had set her mind in a whirl. All sorts of undercurrents and crosscurrents were rumbling about beneath the surface, but she had no idea what they meant or where they would lead. She knew only one thing—that Leyton was right: she had no talent at all for matchmaking.

Nine

With sighs of pleasure and exclamations of gratification, the ladies rose from the dinner table and made their way to the drawing room, as Kelby circulated among the men offering glasses of gleaming red port.

Later, when the men joined the ladies, the guests assorted themselves into groups of two or three. Algy perched on the arm of Beatrice's chair and continued to pour into her sympathetic ear the account of his unhappy childhood, a tale that he'd begun at the table. Horace, unaware that he was being maligned as the cause of his brother's unhappiness, cheerfully thanked Felicia on the magnificence of the meal. This done, he made his way to the love seat where Livy was sitting. To his chagrin he found that he was too late to be able to sit beside her, that place having already been taken by his host. Leyton was quietly complimenting Livy on her appearance, telling her that she should always wear that shade of red. Horace, who would not be outdone, pulled up a chair as close to Livy's other side as he could get and declared loudly that she looked "complete to a shade."

Elaine also was late in achieving her object, for Lord Stoneham had captured George as soon as he appeared in the doorway and engaged him in fond reminiscences about their Cambridge days. Elaine stood a short distance away from them, watching for the moment when their conversation should show signs of waning. But there were no such signs. There were evidently several school events that both men were enthusiastically recalling. Finally Elaine reached the end of her patience. Perfectly aware that she was being rude, she nevertheless broke in on them, interrupting Lord Stoneham's account of an escapade with a barmaid that had both men laughing. She simply came up to them, gave Stoneham a brief nod, took firm hold of George's elbow, and maneuvered him away with such boldness that Lord Stoneham was left agape. Appalled, he strode across the room to his wife. "You may not credit it, my love," he muttered between clenched teeth, "but that pretty Miss Whitmore is a great deal more brazen than one would ever suspect."

Meanwhile, the brazen Miss Whitmore steered her captive to a corner. "I'm very cross with you, my lord," she scolded, but at the same time smiling up at George provocatively. "You were sitting beside me all through dinner, and not once did you mention my gown."

"Your gown?" George asked innocently, removing his elbow from her hold.

"Yes, my gown. I chose it especially for you, you know. I even asked your sister's advice about it. She assured me it was just what you'd like."

"It is just what every man who sees you would like, Miss Whitmore," George said, carefully noncommittal. "A charming gown indeed."

This was not quite the response Elaine wanted, but she pretended to be pleased. "Thank you for the compliment, although it is shockingly belated. But why, my lord, after being my dinner companion not once but twice, do you still call me Miss Whitmore? Let's strike a bargain. If you agree to call me Elaine, I'll agree to drop your title and call you George."

"How can I possibly refuse such an offer?" he asked dryly. Then he made a little bow and started to move away from her.

But she would not be shaken off so easily. Catching hold of his arm, she cooed, "Well then, George, let me hear you take advantage of it."

" 'Advantage,' ma'am?"

"There, you see? You said 'ma'am.' Let me hear you use my given name."

"Very well, ma'am—I mean Elaine. There. I hope that was satisfactory."

"Yes, George, I'm quite pleased. Now we can truly say we are friends." And as if to prove her point, she squeezed his arm fondly.

George, feeling trapped, could think of only one way out. Her possessive grasp of his arm gave him the opportunity to pretend she'd caused his hand to wiggle, thus permitting him to loosen his hold on the stem of the glass he still carried. It tipped over, and the contents splashed all over the front of her gown.

She let out a horrified cry. Everyone in the room looked up.

"Oh, blast!" George exclaimed. "Look what I've done! I've ruined your lovely gown. Elaine, I'm so dreadfully sorry. I'm a clumsy fool."

She stared down at herself, conscious that every eye was taking in the ruin of her costume. The words "*you ARE a clumsy fool*" leaped into her mind, but she didn't say them. She was annoyed with him, but not enough to end the flirtation. "No, you're not," she murmured, but without real conviction. "It was an accident. You mustn't blame yourself."

"Of course he must," declared Felicia, who'd run over to see what she could do. "But don't despair, Elaine, my dear. My Katie will fix it. She can clean anything. And when you get back to town, you will order a brand-new gown and send the bill to Georgie. Right, Georgie?"

"Of course," George said.

"No, no, it's really not necessary," Elaine said in an agony of frustration. "Let's not make a fuss. I'll just go and change." And she ran from the room.

When the others in the room returned their attentions to their former conversations, Felicia turned to her brother with a glare. "You did that on purpose!" she accused.

He gave her an innocent look. "Why do you say that?"

"Because I was watching. You were trying to get away from her, weren't you?"

George shrugged. "Not an easy task, I assure you. I was a bit desperate, but it was a clumsy ruse, I admit."

Felicia sighed. "I know. She's a more determined creature than I imagined her to be. You were right, Georgie, about my friends being—how did you put it?— flirtatiously aggressive."

"Not all of them," George said, turning his eyes toward the love seat where Livy was still sitting.

Felicia followed his glance. "No, no one can call my Livy flirtatious."

"But your Livy seems to have put herself out this evening. Primped herself in fine shape. Good old Horace must have made quite an impression on her."

"Don't be a clunch," his sister sneered. "Livy has no interest in that peacocky bag-pudding."

"I wouldn't be so sure," George said, noting that Livy had turned toward Horace and was listening to him attentively. "She doesn't seem to find him a bag-pudding. Besides, why else would she have taken her hair down and dressed up in red?"

"It wasn't Horace she dressed up for, you bubblehead," Felicia said in the pitying tone one uses for a slow-witted child. "It was for you!"

"For *me*?" He gave a snort of disbelief. "Why on earth would she—?"

"Because she realized you thought of her as a fusty old maid whom I'd invited out of kindness. And she wanted to disabuse you of the notion."

George's jaw dropped. "But I never said such a thing!"

"You didn't have to say it. It was in your face. Even Leyton saw it."

"Good God!"

"Yes, quite!" Felicia said sternly.

George was speechless for a moment. That he could have so cruelly offended the object of his youthful infatuation discomposed him. He did not like to think of himself as unkind. True, his treatment of Elaine might be considered unkind, but that was not the same thing. After all, the immodest chit had brought it on herself. But Miss Olivia Henshaw had done nothing to deserve an insult. She'd only grown older. "Felicia," he muttered, grasping her hands in his, "you must tell her that I never . . . that it's not at all what she . . ." He stopped, realizing that it was a situation he could not explain. "You must apologize for me," he concluded lamely, dropping his hold on her hands.

"I certainly must not," his sister snapped. "You must do it yourself. And right now. Come!"

She pulled him by his arm across the room to the love seat where Livy and her two companions still sat. They stopped speaking and looked up in surprise at the intruders. "Excuse me, Livy dear, for interrupting, but I must take Leyton from you," Felicia explained. "He must help me to persuade Lady Stoneham to play something on the pianoforte for dancing."

"Ah, are we to have some dancing?" Horace asked, rising. "How delightful."

Leyton rose also. "I'm at your service, my love," he assured Felicia, "although you are tearing me away from charming company."

"I'm sorry, Livy, to steal away half your company," Felicia said to her friend, "but I've brought you my brother as a replacement."

"A poor replacement, I'm afraid," George said, bowing.

"Perhaps," Livy said with a smile, "but do sit down, my lord, and we shall see."

Felicia gave her brother a meaningful nudge and went off with her husband. George sat down beside Livy. "If there will be dancing," he said, "I hope you'll stand up with me for the first one."

"I say, Frobisher," Horace cried, "that's a bit cheeky of you! I should have that honor, having been here beside the lady far longer than—"

"Right you are, Horace," came a voice from behind them, and with a trilling laugh, Elaine came floating

round from behind the love seat to reveal herself newly
bedecked in a flowing gown of lilac brocade. "If anyone
deserves her hand, it's you."

Livy's eyebrows rose. "Do you think, Miss Whitmore,
that I'm incapable of deciding for myself who deserves
my hand?"

"I didn't mean that at all," Elaine explained with self-
assured nonchalance. "I only meant that his lordship
couldn't have expected me to change so quickly. If he'd
known I'd be here so soon, I'm sure he would have asked
me for the first dance, wouldn't you, Georgie?"

Helplessly trapped, George pulled himself to his feet.
"Undoubtedly," he said, his mouth tight.

Livy looked up at him with a slightly ironic smile of
sympathy. "Then of course, *Georgie,* your invitation to
me must be rescinded."

"I suppose it must," George said, uncomfortably aware
that she was laughing at him. "I'm so very sorry to have
caused this . . . this imbroglio—"

"You needn't be," Livy assured him, "for after all,
I'm thus spared the embarrassment of having to choose
between two requests."

"Then I can only say thank you for excusing me,"
George said, and with another bow, walked off with
Elaine on his arm.

He did not look at his companion until they'd crossed
the room to the pianoforte, where Lady Stoneham was
riffling through music sheets. Then he glanced down at
the girl on his arm. She was looking quite lovely in her
lilac gown, and she was smiling up at him with a glow
of triumph. "If you're too gentlemanly to thank me,
Georgie, you might at least smile at me," she
prompted.

"In the first place, ma'am, I cannot smile when you
call me Georgie. Only my sister has that right. And in
the second place, for what am I to thank you?"

"For saving you from the necessity of dancing with
that sharp-tongued Miss Henshaw, of course. Don't I deserve even a little smile for that?"

It would be gentlemanly, he supposed, to give her that smile she was begging for, but he had no stomach for gentlemanliness at this moment. It took all his strength to keep from wringing her neck.

Ten

L ady Stoneham played the piano and her husband turned her pages, but everyone else participated in the dancing—a quadrille and three lively country dances. By the end of the last—an animated exercise called Horatio's Fancy—most of the dancers were happy to sit down and catch their breaths. Not so Horace, who went up to Lady Stoneham and asked if she would offer them a waltz.

"If you're going to waltz, Horace," Livy spoke up, "I hope you'll excuse me. I'm quite done in. In fact, with your permission, Felicia, I'm for bed."

George watched her leave with a feeling of desperation. He'd not managed a moment alone with her all evening. But desperation often gives birth to inspiration. "I say, Horace," he said, his eyes lighting up, "if you're set on waltzing, why don't you stand up with Elaine? I'm certain she's up-to-the-mark at waltzing, and we would all take great pleasure in watching you."

The others applauded in agreement. Horace promptly opened his arms to Elaine, who, blushing with pleasure at being the center of attention for something more admirable than a stained dress, stepped into them. As soon as the music started and all eyes were on the dancers, George tiptoed out of the room, dashed across the hallway to the stairs, and caught up with Livy at the second landing. "I say, Miss Henshaw," he said breathlessly, "can you spare me a moment?"

She looked round, her expression changing from surprise to suspicion. "Is it urgent? I am rather tired."

"It's urgent to me." He threw her a pleading look. "We could sit down right here on the stairs—"

"What? Here?" she asked, laughing. "Like a couple of children?"

"Yes, why not?"

"Very well, my lord." She gathered up her skirts, sat down on the top step, and looked up at him bright-eyed, like a little girl waiting for a bedtime story.

He perched on the step below. "Must you keep calling me 'my lord'?" he asked.

"What else shall I call you? Surely you don't wish me to call you Georgie, as so many others do."

"Not so many others. Only Felicia. It's a carryover from childhood."

"I've heard another call you that," she reminded him.

"You mean Miss Whitmore. Yes, but I've put a stop to that." He looked up at her with boyish appeal. "Can't you manage a plain George?"

"Very well, plain George," she responded with a twinkle. "Now, what is the urgent business you wish to talk to me about?"

He hesitated. "This isn't easy. I don't quite know how to start."

"You'd better find a way. I don't intend to sit here hugging my knees for very long."

He took a deep breath. "Very well, here goes. It seems that, at our first meeting, I offended you. I'd like to explain that I—"

Livy's whole body stiffened, and her expression darkened. "Is that your urgent business?"

"Well, yes. I wanted to apologize—"

"To apologize for what, exactly?" she asked, her voice as cold as the look in her eyes.

"For the way I . . . er . . . reacted when I first saw you."

"You want to apologize for that?"

"Yes, I do. I believe my reaction was offensive to you."

She shook her head in disagreement. "But your reaction was spontaneous, was it not?"

He blinked at her, puzzled. "Spontaneous?"

"Yes. It was instinctive, wasn't it? Unguarded? An impulsive response?"

"Yes, of course it was."

"You did not *mean* to hurt me, did you?"

"Of course not."

"Then what reason have you to apologize?"

He ran his fingers through his hair in a gesture of helplessness. "But I *did* hurt you."

She shook her head. "That isn't the point. Your reaction was spontaneous and therefore honest. One must not apologize for an honest act. If I was hurt by it, you are not to blame."

He stared at her for a moment, unsatisfied by the manner in which this conversation was proceeding. His apology had not had the effect he wished for; her cold manner showed she'd not been soothed by it. He wondered if she would be better served by the truth—or something close to the truth. Perhaps he should simply say, *I saw you once, years ago. In my memory you remained young. I was foolishly startled that you had not stayed the same.* Would saying that she'd aged—for that's what his excuse amounted to—be more effective?

Not at all sure this approach would be any better than the other, he nevertheless decided to try. "I don't think you understood my reaction. It was not what you thought."

She glared at him. "Please, my lord, do not repeat—"

"Please, *George,*" he corrected.

She waved away the interruption. "Please, my lord, do not repeat the nonsense about having expected me to be someone else. It was a lame excuse then, and it is now."

Yes, it was a lame excuse, he thought. *And telling her she'd aged would probably not be any better.* "Then all I can say is that I am sorry to have caused you pain, even accidentally," he said in defeat. "I hope you can forgive me."

She stood up. "I thought I made it clear that there was

nothing to forgive, as far as that incident is concerned. It was, after all, a trivial matter that I soon was able to find amusing. But that you should make so great an effort to apologize gives the incident greater significance. It means that you assume *I was cut to the quick by a mere look!* To think of me as so . . . so pathetic—*that,* my lord, is offensive. And that I will not forgive. Good night, my lord."

She turned away from him and walked up the stairs, her head proudly high. Speechless, he watched her go, although every instinct urged him to call her back . . . to say something—anything!—that would make up for his blunder. But what was there to say? *How could you believe I thought of you as pathetic? You were my Venus!* Even if he could say those words, they wouldn't help. They'd only make *him* seem pathetic.

There was nothing else to be done, except to go to bed. He'd get up early and take his leave of this place. He'd had enough—enough of Elaine Whitmore's advances, of Olivia Henshaw's rejections, of his sister's useless advice, and of his own guilt at having behaved like a cad. To be back in London, in plenty of time for Bernard's ball, was just what he needed. Once he'd returned to his proper life, he could forget this entire weekend. In fact he could put his blasted Venus image out of his mind forever.

Strengthened by this new feeling of determination, he got to his feet. "Venus, ha!" he snorted aloud. And he stomped up the stairs to his bedroom and slammed the door.

Eleven

$\mathcal{A}$fter a restless hour of tossing about, George fell into a troubled sleep, his dreams taking him back to a dimly remembered battlefield in Spain. He found himself scrambling up the slope of a ravine as the sound of bullets exploded about his ears. He could sense the enemy right behind him. It seemed urgent that he reach the top of the slope, but hard as he tried, he kept slipping back. After a time, he became aware that a mysterious force was pressing on his shoulder. It seemed intent on pushing him back, no matter how urgently he struggled against it. The pressure grew stronger and stronger until it woke him up. He realized with some relief that he was not on a battlefield but in a bed. The dream faded at once, but, strangely, the pressure on his shoulder did not. Someone was shaking him. Hard.

"Georgie, wake up!"

It was his sister's voice. He opened his eyes. Felicia was standing over him, holding a candle. In the dim light, he could see she'd come from her bed, for she was wearing a nightcap and her silly lilac dressing gown. "Wha's the matter?" he murmured sleepily, rubbing his eyes. "Wha' time 's it?"

"It's half after four. I'm sorry to have to wake you, dearest, but I need you. There's been an emergency."

"Emergency?" George sat up, alarmed. "Has something happened to Leyton?"

"No, no, nothing like that. It's Livy's uncle. He's taken

ill. A messenger came from Scotland ordering her home at once."

George rubbed his eyes to make certain he was awake. "I don't understand. Did you wake me up in the wee hours just to tell me she's leaving? Couldn't this news have kept 'til morning?"

"No, dearest, it couldn't wait. You see, I need you to escort her home."

"Escort her home? To *Scotland*? Are you mad?"

Felicia put a hand to her worried brow. "I don't know what else to do. Leyton cannot do it. He cannot leave when we have a houseful of guests. Nor can we impose such a burden on any of our guests. So, you see, it must be you."

"I don't see! Am I not a guest, too?"

"Yes, but you're family." She dropped down on the bed, facing him. "It won't be so bad, Georgie, honestly it won't. You can take our barouche, and we'll give you Philips to drive. He's an excellent coachman. Livy's uncle's estate is in Lockerbie, just over the border. Philips probably can do the trip in fourteen hours each way."

George bit his lip. He hated to refuse such an urgent request, but he had obligations of his own. "You don't understand, Felicia. I must get back to London. I promised Bernard. I intend to leave this very morning."

His sister's eyes widened in alarm. "But you can't!" she cried. "No one is leaving 'til tomorrow. Are you saying you did not intend to stay?"

"No, I did not."

She looked at him helplessly. "But what am I to do? I can't send my best friend back to Scotland with only her abigail and an elderly coachman to protect her. If anything were to happen, I'd never forgive myself."

George, trying not to let his instinctive sympathy weaken his determination to stick to his own plans, wondered what other means could be used to solve this dilemma. "Who protected her on the trip down?" he inquired.

"She came in her uncle's carriage, with their old family retainer to escort her. He and the carriage were supposed to come back for her on Monday, but evidently they could not be spared in this emergency." She looked up at her brother tearfully. "Georgie, please! Can't you possibly help me in this?"

He met her pleading gaze and sighed in defeat. "I suppose I might. Fourteen hours, you say? If I took my phaeton instead of your carriage, I could probably do it in twelve."

"No, dearest, not the phaeton. Take our carriage. It's heavier and better for long distances."

"But then I'd have to return it to you. If I take my own carriage, I can turn right about in Scotland and make for town. With a few changes of horses and some hard driving, I should—"

Felicia was surprised. "You'd go directly back to London? You'd not come back here?"

"No, of course not. I told you I'm pressed for time. Now, let's see . . . right over the border, you say? If I can figure out—"

"But you can't do that," she objected.

George didn't even hear her. "—I think two days should get me from Scotland back to London in time, if I don't stop."

"But, Georgie, you can't drive for twenty-five or thirty hours without sleep!" his sister cautioned.

He threw his legs over the side of the bed. "Do you want me to escort your friend or not?"

"Yes, but—"

"Then but me no buts. Get out and let me dress."

She threw her arms about his neck. "Oh, Georgie, you're a prince!" she said in a choked voice. "I knew you wouldn't let me down."

"Don't be a wet-goose. What are brothers for?" He released himself from her grasp and turned her to the door. "Ask Kelby to wake my Timmy, will you? Have him ready my phaeton."

She let him propel her over the threshold as she murmured a heartfelt "Thank you, Georgie. I won't forget this."

She was closing the door behind her when her brother called, "Wait!"

She peeped back in. "Yes?"

George had paused in the act of pulling off his nightshirt. "Does your friend Livy know I'll be escorting her?"

"No, not yet."

"She may not wish my escort, you know. She hasn't much liking for me."

"Don't be silly," his sister assured him as she departed. "Everyone likes you."

George snorted bitterly. "Much you know about it," he said to the closed door.

Half an hour later, he came down the stairs, wrapping a wool muffler round his neck. As he descended, he heard some angry whispering from down below. When he came to the top of the last flight of stairs, the voices stopped. Leyton, Felicia, and Livy were gathered in the foyer at the foot of the stairway, and at the sound of his footsteps all of them looked up at him worriedly. "What's amiss?" he asked as he ran down to the bottom.

"It's Livy," Leyton said in disgust. "She refuses to accept your escort."

"Does she, indeed?" George threw his sister a smirk that plainly said *I told you so*.

"I wouldn't dream of imposing on you, my lord," Livy declared. "It is quite unnecessary."

"But, Livy, dearest," Felicia insisted for what must have been the third or fourth time, "you cannot ride for one hundred and twenty miles without a proper escort."

"I not only can, but I will," Livy said, "so send your brother back to his bed and let me be on my way."

"Miss Henshaw," George said with quiet but firm formality, "much as I dislike overruling a lady of your im-

pressive determination, I shall not go back to bed. My
phaeton is at the door. Oblige me, if you please, by stepping outside and getting into it."

"Thank you," she said, lifting her chin stubbornly,
"but I have no intention—"

George took her elbow in a firm grip and propelled
her toward the door. "Not another word on this subject,
ma'am, if you please. The matter is settled."

She tried to wrench free. "But I—"

Still keeping her arm in his grip, he used his free hand
to cover her mouth. "You may not speak unless you
promise it will only be to say good-bye to your hosts."

She sighed in surrender. Feeling her resistance weaken,
George freed her mouth but continued to move her to
the door. She managed to turn her head and cry, "Thank
you, my dears, for everything," before being firmly thrust
out the door and down the stone steps.

A gray dawn was just beginning to light the upper
windows. It offered no promise of warmth. As George
had suspected, this was going to be a cold ride . . . and
in more ways than one. When they reached the carriage,
Livy confirmed his fears by angrily shaking off his grip
and climbing up into it, an air of disapproval enveloping
her like a cloak.

Livy's abigail and Timmy had been standing beside the
carriage shivering in the cold. The abigail was an elderly
woman whose bright keen eyes enlivened a tiny, very
frail form. She seemed so fragile that George was about
to unwrap his muffler and hand it to her when Kelby
came running down carrying a pile of lap robes and a
basket of provisions. The abigail eagerly claimed the
goods and handed Timmy one of the lap robes. Then
George helped her climb up after her mistress. At last
he himself was ready to go. He turned, waved to Felicia
and Leyton, who were standing at the top of the stone
stairway, and promptly leaped aboard.

Timmy was already on the box, the lap robe wrapped
round his shoulders. As soon as he heard George shut
the carriage door, he flicked the horses into action.

Waving and smiling their good-byes, Felicia and Leyton remained on the stairs until the carriage was out of sight. They hoped Livy was smiling back at them, but they very much doubted it.

Twelve

Like Timmy up on the box, the three travelers inside the carriage bundled themselves in their lap robes to ward off the chill. After wrapping the robe about her shoulders, Livy, on the rear seat, turned her attention to her window. Her abigail, seated beside her, could not stop shivering. "Michty me," the elderly woman muttered, " 'tis unco' chittery."

"What did you say?" George asked from the front seat. Since both seat benches in the phaeton faced front, he had to turn his head to see her.

"She says it's unusually cold," Livy explained without shifting her gaze from the passing landscape. "My Bridie speaks the Lowland tongue."

"Your Bridie is quite right, no matter what her tongue. January weather seems to have found its way into November." He unwound the muffler from his neck. "Here, Bridie," he said to the abigail, "put this on."

At those words, Livy turned from the window. "No, Bridie, don't take it. We've imposed on his lordship quite enough."

The abigail, with the muffler in her hand, hesitated.

"Let her have it, ma'am," George insisted. "She's older than we, after all, and older people feel the cold more than we do. Besides, I can put up my coat collar."

Livy glanced at her shivering maid and gave in. "Very well, my lord. Thank you."

"Aye, m' lor'. I do thankee," Bridie said, and promptly

pulled the muffler over her head and ears and wound the rest round her neck.

Livy returned to gazing out the window. Bridie, after flicking a narrow-eyed glance from her mistress to his lordship and back again, cuddled into the corner of the carriage and went to sleep.

They rode this way for a long while. The only sounds were Bridie's snores, the wind that rattled the windows, and the clip-clop of the horses' hooves. At last George could bear it no longer. Turning about in his seat, he said, "I wonder, ma'am, if you intend for us to ride in this awkward silence all the way to Scotland."

Her only answer was to pull the lap robe closer about her and shift her position away from him. Under her hood, she was wearing some sort of lace-edged cap—he believed it was called a widow's cap, but it was also worn by unmarried females who'd given up hope of wedlock—that fell over her forehead and edged her cheeks. Turned away from him as she was, the deuced cap made it impossible to see her face.

"I know you're angry with me," George persisted, "though I'm in some confusion as to why. Is it because of my reprehensible behavior toward you at Felicia's? Or is it my temerity in insisting on escorting you home?"

Hearing a plaintive note in his voice, she looked over her shoulder at him. "Neither," she said. Then, correcting herself, she added, "Or both."

"Well, which is it?" he wanted to know.

"Oh, I don't know." With a helpless shrug, she turned to face him. "I suppose I ought to be grateful to you."

"For escorting you home? I should say so!" He glowered at her in mock accusation. "It's taking me twenty-eight hours out of my way."

"Well, you needn't blame me. I didn't ask for your escort."

"I don't blame you. It was a necessary duty, and I was the logical one to perform it. Like it or no, you had to have an escort. We both may as well accept it with good grace."

"Yes, you're right, of course," she admitted, dropping her eyes. "I've been churlish."

"Yes, you have," he said cheerfully.

Her head came up at once. "Don't mistake for one moment that this changes anything between us," she warned.

"Doesn't it?" he asked innocently.

"Your taking this trouble in my behalf does not override my dislike of your overbearing behavior."

This surprised him. "Do you really find me overbearing?" he asked bluntly.

"Can you doubt it, after you thrust me into this carriage against my will?" She paused for a moment, her brow wrinkled thoughtfully. "Of course, your offering your muffler to Bridie was an act of kindness. It confuses me, I admit. But such a minor act is hardly enough to offset my impression that you are autocratic and presumptuous."

He rubbed his chin, wondering how to respond. Convinced that he was not at all like the person she described, he was more amused than offended. "Autocratic and presumptuous, am I?" he asked, raising an eyebrow in disbelief. "That's very strange."

"Why strange?"

"Because Felicia assures me that everyone likes me."

A laugh bubbled out of her. "Really? *Everyone?*"

"Yes, everyone." Having won a laugh from her, he swiveled about on the seat, stretched his legs up on it, and rested his arm along the back so that he could more comfortably look at her.

She was studying him thoughtfully, as if she were measuring what degree of truth there might be in Felicia's claim. "At the risk of adding to your already enormous conceit, my lord, I admit that Felicia may be right."

"Right about everyone liking me? Nonsense! You don't believe I take seriously my sister's affectionate flattery."

"Yet there is some truth to it. At least about young

women liking you. From what I hear, they all do seem
to flock about you."

"No, they don't. But even if they did, it doesn't count.
It's not me they like. It's my title and my ten thousand
a year."

"I wouldn't say that. You are quite prepossessing, you
know, even without the title and wealth."

"But autocratic and presumptuous," he reminded her.

"Yes."

"And conceited."

"Yes."

"Hmmm," was all he said.

"But my views are not typical," she said comfortingly,
feeling that perhaps she'd gone too far. "After all, I'm
not a young woman."

"Young enough, ma'am, to cause your views of me to
sting." He clutched his chest in extravagant distress.
"You cut me to the quick."

"A likely tale," she scoffed. "As if my views can matter against so many."

"But they do," he said, suddenly serious. "They do."
The sincerity he heard in his own voice surprised him.
The rest of their conversation had all been banter, but
it came as a shock to realize that he'd really meant what
he just said. He cared about what she thought of him.
He cared a great deal. But why? She was a far cry from
the Venus of his dreams—that much was definitely decided. So why should he give a tinker's damn what she
thought of him?

Thirteen

*G*eorge had hoped that, by late afternoon, they would have arrived at their destination, but here it was past three, and—according to Livy, who knew the road well— they were still three or four hours from her home. George realized that he'd greatly underestimated the speed he could make. There were several reasons his well-sprung phaeton was not living up to its potential: for one thing, the sky had been dark all day and the weather unseasonably cold, making visibility poor and driving uncomfortable. He and Timmy had taken turns sitting up on the box, changing their positions every two hours, but that had not helped. Then there were the horses. They'd changed horses at two posting inns thus far, but at the first stop they'd been given a pair of slugs. One could not hope for ten-mile-an-hour speed from such inadequate animals. The young bays they'd managed to acquire at their last stop half an hour ago seemed more promising, but now a light snow was falling, and in the waning daylight, George, who was up on the box, could hardly see the edges of the road.

He was asking himself if it would be possible to proceed once darkness fell, when there was a dreadful crunching sound. The carriage lurched hideously to his right, wobbled a bit, and then the right corner of the coach crashed down. The horses dragged it a foot or two before he could pull them to a stop. It was obvious that they'd hit some crevice in the road, and that the right

front wheel had given way. He jumped down to see the
extent of the damage.

A much heavier snow was falling now. There was already a white blanket covering the landscape. George
saw that the wheel had sunk into a snowdrift. He had to
sweep some of the snow away with his hands. He discovered that the wheel was beyond repair. Every spoke had
been broken by the wheel's having been dragged a few
feet after the initial break. "Blast it!" he cursed aloud.

By this time, Timmy and the two women had emerged
from the tilted carriage. "We're hobbled, sure as check,"
Timmy muttered after a quick look.

George nodded. "There's only one thing to be done.
We'll unhitch the horses and ride back with the ladies
to the posting inn. Miss Henshaw and Bridie can warm
up with some hot toddies while you and I come back
here with a new wheel." He looked up at the sky and
then at Livy. "Unless . . ."

"Yes?" she asked, taking note of the worry in his eyes.

"Unless you agree to put off the repairs 'til morning."

Livy bit her lip. "My uncle will be livid. I'm sure he's
expecting me to be walking in the door at any moment."

"But you see, ma'am, by the time we replace the
wheel, it'll be dark. And if the snow continues to fall,
I'll be hard-pressed to see the roadway."

"You're right, of course," she said with a discouraged
sigh. "Let's start back to the inn, as you suggest. If by
that time there is no sign of clearing, we'll do as you say
and put up there for the night."

The agreement made, Timmy went off to unhitch the
horses. George continued to study the broken wheel. "I
wonder if there's some other damage," he muttered. "I'd
better take a look underneath and make sure the axle is
still sound."

He lay down on his back upon the snow blanket and
slid under the tilted carriage. "Everything seems to be—"
he began, when one of the horses Timmy was untying
reared up on its hind legs, pulling on the reins that tied it
to the phaeton. The carriage shook, the rear right wheel

cracked, and the rear of the carriage gave way, pinning George down at the hipline.

Livy gasped and clapped her hands to her mouth in terror.

Bridie screamed, "Michty me!"

Timmy came running round from the front, took one look at the pair of legs sticking out from under the tilted carriage, and cried out in horror, "Oh, m'lord, I've *killed* ye!"

A voice came from below. "No, no. I'm alright. I just can't . . . move."

"Can't move?" Timmy knelt down beside the legs. "Blimee! 'Ave ye broken yer back?"

"No," came George's voice, "I'm all right, I think."

Livy knelt opposite Timmy. "Move your legs, my lord, if you can," she called under the carriage to him.

The booted feet wiggled and, slowly, the knees came up. "There," George said.

"Can you move your arms, too?" Livy asked.

"Yes, though there's not much room. I seem to be pinned down here."

Timmy got up and pushed against the side of the phaeton. "The deuced carriage can't be budged," he muttered.

"Couldn't we dig him out?" Livy asked, getting to her feet.

"Even if I 'ad a shovel, which I ain't," the tiger said, kicking at the ground under the snow, "the ground's frozen solid. If there wasn't a drift o' snow on the ground, 'is lordship'd be crushed fer certain."

Livy paced about for a moment, studying the situation. Then she turned to Timmy. "Have you any rope?"

"That I 'ave," the tiger said, his face lighting with hope. "A coil of it, under the box. What was ye thinkin'?"

"I'm thinking that we could tie it round the frame of the door up there, bring the horses round to the side, attach them to the rope, and have them pull the carriage up."

"It wouldn't work," George called out from below. "They'd pull the door off its hinges before they could budge this damn weight off the ground."

There was a discouraging silence for a moment. Then George spoke again. "Is Timmy nearby?"

"Yes, m'lord," Timmy said, kneeling down close to the carriage frame.

"Put the women and yourself on the horses and get to the inn," George ordered. "Then send as many men as you can find back here to lift this damn carriage off me."

"No!" Livy said decidedly. "We will not leave you here alone."

"Yes, you will," George shouted angrily. "For once, woman, do as you're told."

"Be still, will you? I have another plan." She knelt down close to the carriage frame. "Why couldn't we pull the rope through the windows of both doors and loop it up over the roof?" she asked the imprisoned George. "The horses couldn't pull the roof off, could they? They'd only have to lift it a few inches off the ground . . . just enough to give us room to pull you out."

"It might work," George granted. "You could try."

Timmy immediately ran to the box and got the rope. Livy climbed up to the left-side door—which was now like an angled roof—and passed the rope through the window to the right-side window, under which Bridie was waiting to catch it. Then the maid tossed her end over the top, where Livy caught it and handed both ends to Timmy, who had brought both horses round to the side.

As he tied both ends of the rope to the horses' collars and saddle straps, Livy ran back to George's legs. "We're ready," she told him, "but don't move until I give the word." She waved to Timmy, who took hold of the bridles and slowly urged the horses forward.

The rope tightened as the horses strained forward, and then the carriage creaked. "Slowly!" Livy shouted to Timmy. "It's coming."

The carriage frame began to lift from the ground, inch by creaking inch. When it lifted about a hand span above

George's body, she shouted "Stop!" She and Bridie each took a leg and gently pulled. After a moment, George, using his elbows, helped them to haul him out.

"He's out!" she shouted to Timmy. "You can ease off now."

"Praise be!" Timmy shouted back as he eased his hold on the horses and let the carriage fall back down.

Meanwhile, Livy was helping George to his feet. "Do you think you can stand?" she asked, releasing her hold on him. George straightened up and took a few steps. "There!" he said, grinning. "I'm fine." And then a knee gave way.

"Oh, my dear!" Livy cried, grasping him under his arms.

"No, it's nothing," he assured her, shaking off her hold and getting up again. "It's my hip. It's probably nothing more than a bruise. I can walk." And to prove it, he limped in a circle around her.

"Oh, Georgie!" she said with a tearful laugh and threw her arms around him. "I'm so relieved."

He held her for a moment before taking her arms from his neck and holding her off. "What did you call me?"

She didn't understand what he'd said. "What?" she asked.

"You called me Georgie!" he accused.

"Oh." She brushed a tear from her cheek and smiled. "Well, Felicia always calls you that. I've become used to thinking of you that way. I'm sorry."

"Don't be. I think I like it when you say it. Do you think, now that you've saved my life, that I may call you Livy, as Felicia does?"

"Of course you may. But I did not save your life. You're only bruised."

"But if not for your quick thinking, I might have had to lie there in the snow for hours. I might very well have frozen to death." He lifted her hand to his lips. "You, Livy, are a very remarkable woman."

Livy, unaccustomed to gallantry, snatched her hand away in embarrassment. "Don't be so silly. Instead of standing about speaking nonsense, we should be making our way back to the inn."

George could not but agree. In a very few moments, the horses were brought round, and with Timmy and Bridie on one and George and Livy on the other, they made their way carefully through the snow and the darkness toward the promise of shelter.

Fourteen

$\mathcal{A}$t that moment, in London, Bernard was wheeling himself over to the window to draw the curtains for the night. To his horror, he saw that snowflakes were beginning to fall. "Dash it, George, why aren't you back?" he cried aloud. "If this is a storm coming down from the north, you'll never make it now!"

His man, Pratkin, knocked at the door. *The blasted fellow must have heard me,* Bernard thought in annoyance. "Come in," he grunted, making his disgust clear in his tone.

"Sorry to disturb you, sir, but—" the valet began as he closed the door carefully behind him.

"You're not a bit sorry," Bernard said belligerently, wheeling his chair about to face the intruder. The movement was so abrupt that the lap robe over his knees slipped to the floor. "You know perfectly well that I wanted to be left alone."

"Yes, sir, but you see, there's—"

"There's always a but, isn't there, Pratkin, when you want your own way?"

Pratkin had been Bernard's valet too long to be disturbed by his master's moods. "Since when do I ever get my own way?" he retorted calmly as he picked up the lap robe and spread it over Bernard's knees.

"When *don't* you get your own way? Do you think I'm such a fool that I don't know how you rule the roost?"

Pratkin merely rolled his eyes heavenward. "Be that

as it may, sir, I came up for a reason. I think you should ask me why."

"To annoy me, that's why." Bernard turned his chair around toward his desk.

"To tell you that you have a visitor," Pratkin said.

The wheelchair stopped. "A visitor?" Bernard wheeled about again, his face lighting up hopefully. "It's not—?"

"No, sir, it's not Lord Chadleigh. He wouldn't wait to be announced. It's a lady come to see you."

Bernard paled. "A *lady*? Who on earth—?"

"It's Miss Renwood," Pratkin said, a glint in his eyes belying the impassivity of his face.

"Miss Renwood?" Bernard was completely taken aback. "Do you mean *Harriet*? Good God! Harriet, *here*? *Now*?"

"Yes, sir, here and now. Shall I show her up?"

"Well, of course show her up! You blasted idiot, how could you have stood there bantering all this while when she's been waiting downstairs?" He ran his fingers through his hair in perturbation. "Hurry down at once!"

"Yes, sir," Pratkin said, and went promptly toward the door.

"Wait!" Bernard wheeled himself toward his valet, his color now flushed and his eyes terrified. "Do you think this shabby old coat is . . . ? Perhaps I should get up on my crutches and put on that silk dressing gown."

Pratkin's enigmatic expression gave way to an affectionate smile. "You look fine, sir, just the way you are."

Bernard, feeling foolish, murmured, "Thank you, Pratkin," and returned his man's smile with a self-deprecating grin of his own.

He had only time to smooth back his unruly hair when Harriet appeared in the doorway. Pratkin had evidently taken her wrap, but she still wore a green chip hat perched on her red curls, a hat Bernard believed to be completely inadequate for a snowy evening but making her look quite delectable. "Good evening," he managed to gulp.

"Good evening, Bernard," she said with a somewhat naughty smile. "Are you shocked at my calling on you this way?"

"No, no, of course not . . ." he began, but his innate honesty would not permit him to lie. "Well, yes, I *am* shocked, if truth be told."

"Yes, naturally you are," she said complacently. "Mama was, too, when I told her I was coming."

"Are you saying that Lady Redwood gave you permission to visit a bachelor in his rooms?" Bernard demanded, appalled.

"I didn't ask her permission," the girl said, stepping over the threshold and looking about the room with interest. "I just informed her of my intention. I admit that Mama made a mild objection, but she knew I'd not heed it."

"Why did you not heed it?"

"Really, Bernard, what a silly question." She circled about the room, studying the titles of his books and the pictures on his walls. "Mama and I both know that you are a gentleman of the highest principles and that I am in no danger in calling on you."

Bernard frowned. "I suppose that much is true. Though not very flattering to my sense of my manhood."

"Oh, bosh! This has nothing to do with your manhood. It's your sense of honor that makes you safe to visit. And, to be sure, my maid is downstairs. If it would be soothing to your offended sense of your manhood, I can call her up to sit with us."

"That won't be necessary." He motioned her to an armchair before the fire. "Sit down, do."

She nodded and went to the chair, gathering up the skirts of her striped green-and-black muslin gown and slipping into the large chair with such grace that he shivered with pleasure at the sight. But taking himself in hand, he wheeled himself across the room to face her. "Now, tell me, Miss Renwood, what is so important as to cause you to undertake this daring act of misconduct?"

"Does the fact that I've done something daring mean

that you can no longer call me Harriet?" she asked, fluttering her lashes at him.

"Come, girl, don't play games. Why are you here?"

"It's about Mama's ball," she said, becoming serious. "Ever since you told us, the other day on the street, that you were not certain of attending, I've been concerned that you would be cowardly and not come if your friend Frobisher does not return on time. Has he returned, by the way?"

"No, not yet."

"And you're still adamant about not coming without him?"

"I'm afraid so."

"Then I'm glad I undertook this 'daring act of misconduct.' I have a solution to your problem. My brother Denny."

He blinked. "Your brother?"

"Yes. I've spoken to him, and he'd be delighted to take Frobisher's place at your side."

Bernard stiffened. "Indeed?"

"Yes, truly." She leaned forward eagerly. "Isn't that a perfect solution?"

"You brother is, I believe, sixteen years old, is that right?" he asked coldly.

"Yes."

"And, like any red-blooded youngster, has a profound dislike for balls?"

"Yes, but—"

"Then how, I'd like to know, was he persuaded to be 'delighted' to accompany me—an old codger on crutches whom he barely knows—to a social event he is bound to detest?"

This icy response surprised and confused her. "Old codger? You can't believe . . . My brother doesn't . . . You mustn't think . . ." In sudden alarm that she'd blundered somehow, her chin began to tremble.

The trembling chin was very appealing, but Bernard did not relent. "Tell me, Miss Renwood, how the boy was coerced into agreeing to this exciting treat. Did you threaten to keep him from attending his school's prize cricket match? Or to send him to visit his least favorite aunt for Christmas? Or to make him eat sprouts every meal for a month?"

She lifted her head proudly. "None of those things."

"Let's be honest, girl. No red-blooded young fellow would have agreed to such an onerous task without some sort of threat."

"It wasn't a threat." She dropped her eyes from his intense stare. "It was a bribe."

"Aha! And how did you bribe him?"

She sighed in defeat. "I promised I'd buy him the Spanish filly he wants so badly."

"How very generous of you." He turned his chair away from her and remained silent for a long moment. When at last he spoke again, it was in a low, subdued voice. "I'm sorry, Harriet, but I'm sure you won't be surprised to learn that I'm refusing your offer."

"I don't see why. Please, Bernard, be reasonable. It won't hurt Denny to spend an evening in your company."

"It would, however, hurt me."

She stared at him for a long moment and then got slowly to her feet. "I've offended you, haven't I?" she asked, walking round his chair and looking down at him.

"I'm afraid so."

"I see." She gulped back the tears that were suddenly choking her. "Offending you was the last thing I wanted to do." She took a deep breath. "But I shall not apologize," she said and, swinging round on her heel, strode briskly to the door. There she paused and turned back to him. "It seems, Sir Bernard Tretheway, that I've been quite wrong about you."

He looked over his shoulder at her. "In what way?"

"I believed you to be a man of sense," she said, her voice deepened with her unshed tears, "but no man of sense would take offense at what I've said and done. In fact, it would occur to any man of sense to wonder *why* a young woman would plead with him on the street, would bribe her brother to escort him, and would undertake this daring act of misconduct just to get him to attend a foolish little social affair. And if this man of sense should determine the answer, I believe he would regret to his dying day his rejection of the invitation. But since you are evidently not a man of sense, I needn't concern myself that you'll suffer any regrets. Good night, sir."

She shut the door behind her with a loud finality. He gaped at it, trying to guess what it was she was trying to say to him. He *did* have sense enough to wonder why she'd pleaded with him that morning on the street, why she'd bribed her brother, and why she'd come to his rooms this evening. She was certainly going to extraordinary lengths to convince him to attend a ball that she herself had called "a foolish little social affair." Why?

He knew she liked him a bit. But could it be that she felt more than mere liking? Could she be trying to tell him that she *cared* for him? Could she care for a foolish, crippled, cowardly fellow like himself?

No. It wasn't possible. She was just being kind.

Or was she?

In an agony of confusion, he wheeled himself back to the window and stared out at the snow, trying to calm the emotions that Harriet's visit had set into disarray. He was usually a levelheaded fellow, accustomed to handling the limitations of his impairment with good sense, but when it came to his feelings for Harriet, he was on unfamiliar ground. He found his mood swinging wildly from excitement (*Can she possibly love me?*) to despair (*She's probably only feeling sorry for me*). And staring out the window did nothing to appease him. "Damnation, George, I need you! Where are you?" he cried out to the unheeding snowflakes.

Fifteen

George was also gazing out at the snow. From the window of the taproom of the quaint old inn into which they'd stumbled, weary and half frozen, he could see the flakes coming down thick and fast. His promise to Bernard nagged at him. He stood there at the window muttering curses. He cursed at the snow, at the broken wheels, at his sister for getting him into this scrape, and at himself for ever having given in to the temptation to see his Venus in the first place. He should have stayed in London, as Bernard had urged. He'd been a blasted fool.

More than three days remained before the Renwood ball. It was, he hoped, still possible to keep that promise. He'd already convinced the innkeeper to send the ostler and two stablemen out at dawn to replace the wheels. If they could right the carriage quickly, he could start out early and reach Livy's home by midafternoon. Then he could take off immediately for London. He might yet make it. But this damnable snowfall made the prospect look dim.

A stirring at the doorway made him look round. Livy had come down from the inn's only guest room, where she'd gone to try to dry her garments at the fire. "Is it still coming down?" she asked.

He stared at her. She'd removed the widow's cap that she'd worn all day and had shaken down her hair. It now fell in charming disarray about her shoulders. It was not a dull brown as it had appeared when he first saw her but a shining auburn, thick and temptingly touchable. Her cheeks were flushed, probably because of having been close to the fire. Her lips, not pressed together as they'd been when he first saw her, seemed full and luscious. And then there was the matter of her figure. The simple lavender muslin gown she was wearing was still damp, and it clung to her in such a manner that it was quite obvious she was not nearly as gaunt as he'd once thought. She looked—he had to admit it—quite lovely. If she'd looked that way when he'd first seen her, he might not have been so greatly disappointed.

She crossed the room and joined him at the window. "It's still coming down, I see," she said worriedly. "We shall have to put up here for the night, that much is clear."

"We've no choice," he said. "I couldn't ask the stablemen to work on the carriage tonight, not in this weather."

"No, of course you couldn't," Livy agreed, "but I don't know how we shall manage to sleep."

"I've thought of that. The innkeeper tells me that he can put up a cot for Bridie in the bedroom with you, and Timmy has arranged to bunk with the ostler, so we shall manage. We shall all have to sleep in our clothes, of course."

"But what about you?" she asked. "Where will you sleep?"

"I'll sleep here, on a chair near the fire."

"Oh, no!" she cried. "That won't do at all. Not after what you've been through today."

"I'll be fine," he assured her with a smile. "I can sleep anywhere. I've slept in much worse places when I was fighting in Spain. Come and sit down. I've ordered dinner. I hope you can stomach a mutton stew."

The stew, as it happened, was delicious. And afterward, the innkeeper brought in two rum toddies, which he heated by plunging a red-hot poker into the mugs.

Sipping the steaming brew brought them both to a state of dreamy relaxation. Leaning back in her chair, Livy asked him questions about his adventures in Spain. He enjoyed telling her about the battles, his near escapes, and the time he came face-to-face with Wellington himself. It was a very pleasant evening. When the mantel clock struck midnight, and she stood up and bid him good night, he was sorry to see it end.

The innkeeper came in and banked the fire. Timmy popped his head in to say good night. And then George was alone. He pulled a chair to the fire, propped his feet up on the fireplace fender, and tried to sleep. But his hip pained him, and no matter how he tried to settle himself, he could not find a comfortable position. Unable to fall asleep, his thoughts began to circle about Livy. Though she'd not turned out to be his Venus, she was nevertheless an admirable, resolute, plucky sort of female. And ingenious, too. If it hadn't been for her quick thinking, he might still be lying out there in the snow, pinned under the carriage, and if not actually freezing to death, at the very least suffering from frostbitten legs. What was more, she had not turned out to be the spinsterish creature he'd expected from that early glimpse of her. He'd made a hasty misjudgment. He'd been put off by pursed lips, a pallid face, and a topknot of hair. *I ought to learn,* he told himself, *not to jump to hasty conclusions based on trivial . . .*

The next thing he knew, he was being shaken by the shoulder. "Wake up, yer lordship," Timmy was saying. "The new wheels is on. Ye cin look fer yerself. I drove the carriage right up t' the door."

George opened his eyes. The early-morning sunshine, brightened by the snowy covering that blanketed the landscape, was streaming in through the window. "Good God," he said, blinking, "what time is it?"

"Almost seven. I think Miss Henshaw's comin' down."

George winced, not only from the pain in his sore hip but from the stiffness in every other part of his body. Groaning, he pulled himself to his feet. He'd just managed to straighten up when Livy and Bridie bustled in. "I hope you're ready to leave, my lord," Livy said urgently. "I see that the carriage is right outside, waiting for us."

George studied her in some surprise. This was not the same Livy to whom he'd bid good night just a few hours before. With her widow's cap now set snugly over her hair, her face pale, and her lips pressed tightly together, she was again the spinster he'd first seen. He noticed, too, that the hands clasping her cloak to her neck were trembling with agitation. "Is something wrong, Livy?" he asked.

She shook her head. "It's only that we're so very late. My uncle will be beside himself."

"In concern for your safety?"

Bridie let out a mirthless laugh. "Huh!" she said scornfully.

Livy threw her a dagger look. "No, my lord," she said as she started out. "It's just that . . . that he doesn't like being kept waiting."

"Out o' doot `'e don't," Bridie muttered in what George took to be a phrase of emphatic agreement.

"Is he a curmudgeon?" George asked. "Is that why you're in a taking?"

"I'm not in a taking," Livy said impatiently from the doorway. "The innkeeper's wife has given us a basket of tidbits to take with us for our breakfast, so do come along."

As he followed the ladies out to the carriage, George wondered what could account for the change in Livy's manner since the night before. Her tension was palpable. Was it because of her uncle? Was she worried about his health? Or was she fearful—as Bridie's attitude seemed to suggest—of incurring his anger? *How strange,* he thought. Livy had proved herself to be a resolute— nay, even a formidable—female. If the prospect of an uncle's displeasure could so greatly discompose a woman like that, what sort of monstrous fellow must he be?

But, he reminded himself, this question had best not be asked. He didn't want to know. He could not become involved. He had a pressing obligation back in London. Livy's problems were no concern of his.

Sixteen

*I*t was blue skies all the way to Scotland, making the snowy landscape seem almost cheerful. Inside the carriage, however, a painful silence reigned. No matter how hard he tried, George could not coax any response from Livy other than a monosyllabic yes or no. After a couple of hours, he left the comfort of the carriage and took over the reins from Timmy. He remained on the box for the rest of the trip.

As they crossed the border into Scotland, the weather worsened. It seemed as if the sky had a border, too, separating a sunny English sky from a dour and threatening Scottish one. As the carriage rumbled up and down the Scottish hills, snow began to fall, the flakes blowing wildly about in an icy wind. It was obvious that a real storm was on its way. For the last few miles of the trip, the going was difficult. By the time they reached Henshaw Castle in Lockerbie, the day was darkening, the snow was falling heavily, and the wind was fierce. George, who'd intended to turn the phaeton about and head south just as soon as he'd brought Livy to her door, realized that his plan could not work. Driving any longer in this weather was out of the question.

Livy did not wait to see what he would do. As soon as the carriage stopped at the entrance of Henshaw Castle, she leaped out and, ignoring the buffeting wind, ran up the stone steps and disappeared inside. It was Bridie who took command. "Harken, m'lord," she ordered as

soon as she and Timmy had climbed out of the carriage
and George had come down from the box, "gang ye up
inside, belyne!" And she pushed him toward the stairs
and turned to Timmy.

George understood that she meant for him to go up
into the castle, but he remained where he was, watching
with admiration as the tiny creature, with a series of
indistinguishable words but very explicit hand gestures,
made it clear to Timmy where to take the horses.

As soon as Timmy set off, Bridie turned again to
George. The diminutive abigail pushed him up the stairs
ahead of her, like a disgruntled mother dealing with a
recalcitrant (though oversized) son. He almost expected
her to take him by the ear.

Because of the wind's blowing thick snowflakes into
his face, George could barely discern the details of the
exterior of the building. All he could see was a looming
grayness, but it was enough for him to get an impression
of age and decay. Therefore, when he entered the house,
the appearance of the entry hall did not surprise him. It
was as dark and gloomy as he expected. There were several candle sconces on the walls but only one held a lit
candle. In the dim light, he could see that the stone floor
was only partially covered with a shabby carpet and that
the few paintings on the walls were portraits of darkly
dressed, glowering old men. It was a far from welcoming scene.

Before he was able to shake the snow from his greatcoat, a grizzled old manservant approached him. "Lord
Chadleigh?" he asked, awkwardly helping George off
with his coat, "Miss Livy sends her apologies for leavin'
ye so abruptly and begs ye'll make yersel' comfortable
in the sittin' room. If ye'll follow me . . ."

Before leading the way, however, he murmured to Bridie that she was wanted upstairs. The little abigail, with
a nod to George, scampered off up a huge staircase,
pulling off her cloak as she ran.

George followed the man down a dark corridor. The
old fellow's legs were misshapen, and he walked as if

every step pained him. George came up beside him. "I take it that you're the butler," he remarked, slowing his pace to indicate that the servant needn't hurry.

"Yes, m' lord. I be McTavish, at yer service."

"I hope, McTavish, that someone is taking care of my man?"

"Oh, aye, m'lord. Our coachman is helpin' him stable the horses. And Mrs. Nicol, our housekeeper, will see to providin' him some warm food and a room."

They had reached the sitting room, a cheerier place because of a fire burning in the fireplace and a lighted oil lamp on a table near the room's one narrow window. "May I get ye somethin' to drink, m'lord?" the butler asked. "A dram of Scottish whisky, perhaps, to warm ye?"

"Yes, that would be—"

A sudden noise—like someone shouting, but from some distance away—caught George by surprise. "What was that?" he asked.

The butler rolled his eyes in annoyance. "I must go, m'lord," he said, hobbling on his shaky legs to the door. "I'll be back with yer drink soon as I can." And he was gone.

The shouting continued for a long time, although George could not distinguish any words. When silence at last fell, George expected to see the butler with his drink, but no one appeared. He paced about the room, feeling a mounting impatience. Finally, having nothing to do and no one to discuss what arrangements were being made for his accommodation, he decided to explore his surroundings for himself. His first objective was to find Timmy, ensure his comfort, and discuss plans for them to make their escape as soon as possible.

He wandered about, down one corridor and up another, glancing into the rooms he passed along the way. In one room, which he took to be a drawing room, the furnishings were covered with sheets. Another room was unmistakably a library. The tables and chairs were not covered with dust sheets, but there was no fire burning

in the hearth. Why, he wondered, did everything seem
so unused?

At last he found a back stairway leading down. He
descended and, following the smell of baking bread, soon
located the servants' dining room. He paused in the
doorway. Inside, Timmy sat at the end of a long table,
eating some bread and cheese. A housemaid was just
entering from the kitchen with a steaming pot of tea and
a mug. At the sight of George in the doorway, she
gasped.

Timmy looked up. "Yer lordship!" he cried, jumping
to his feet. "I been wonderin' where they were hidin'
ye."

"Sit down, man, sit down," George said, entering. "I
was wondering the same about you." He dropped down
on a chair beside Timmy and looked up at the maid,
who was gaping at him in astonishment. "If that's some
hot tea," he said to her, "I'd be obliged if you'd get me
a cup. I'm chilled through."

Nervously, she immediately set the pot and mug in
front of him.

"No, that's for my man," George told her, pushing the
tea things over to Timmy. "Can you get a cup for me?"

The overwhelmed maid, who'd never before come
face-to-face with a "nob"—and down here belowstairs,
no less!—merely gulped, nodded, and hurried off.

Timmy looked after her with a leer, for the girl was a
shapely little morsel. Then he turned back to George,
shaking his head in disgust. "I ain't never seen a place
like this'n afore," he said. " 'Ere is this big table, wi'
seats fer at least a dozen, but there's mebbe six on the
staff o' this entire 'ouse."

"Six? Is that all?" George asked. "Are you sure?"

"There's McTavish the butler," Timmy said, counting
on his fingers, "an' the coachman—Mr. Shotton is 'is
name, an' 'e tole me there's no one but 'im workin' in
the stables—an' I think Sir Andrew, Miz Henshaw's
uncle, might 'ave a valet, an' there's Bridie, o' course,
an' the 'ousekeeper, Mrs. Nicol. That's five. An' 'er"—

he jerked his thumb in the direction in which the maid
had disappeared, the scull'ry—" 'er name's Peggy."

"It hasn't taken you long to learn pretty Peggy's
name," George teased.

Timmy laughed. "No one's ever called Timmy Noakes
a slow-top. But they've got 'er runnin' about so busy I
cain't get 'er alone fer a second."

"I'm not surprised, with only six in help. This house
in enormous. Leyton Abbey isn't as large as this, and
they have a staff of twenty or more," George mused,
half to himself. "I don't see how they can manage here."

"I don't neither," Timmy said. "Mus' be that this 'ere
Sir Andrew is tight wi' 'is brass."

"Perhaps," George said with a dismissive wave, feeling
uncomfortable about speaking ill of his host, "but that's
not why I came looking for you. First of all, I want to
know if you're being treated well."

Timmy shrugged. "Well enough, I s'ppose. My room
'as a fire an' a decent bed." His eyes gleamed mischievously. "An' wi' any luck, big enough fer two."

"Good, then. You'd best work quickly, for we're here
only for one night, after all. That is, if the weather clears.
I'd like to leave tomorrow, if at all possible."

"I dunno," Timmy said doubtfully and pointed at
something behind George's head. "Look at that."

George turned to look. What Timmy had indicated
was a little window, high on the wall behind him. It was
almost completely covered with snow. "Oh, blast!"
George swore. "The roads will probably be impassable
tomorrow."

It was dispiriting to realize that he might have to spend
more than one night in this ramshackle place. Even the
mug of steaming-hot tea that the pretty scullery maid set
before him could not dispel the feeling of gloom that
overwhelmed him. What troubled him most was that he
was helpless to do anything—either about the weather
or his depressing surroundings. There was nothing he
could do but return upstairs to find the butler. In his
state of frustration, he wanted nothing more than to

throw himself on a soft mattress, bury himself under a comforter, and forget his misery in sleep. He could only hope that he, too, would be given a room with a fire and a decent bed.

Seventeen

*T*o his surprise, his room, when he was finally brought to it, was rather splendid. It was in a tower, with windows surrounding him on three sides. The view, he thought, would be vast and probably magnificent once the storm had cleared and visibility restored. The one windowless wall held a large fireplace, a wardrobe, and a huge, canopied bed fitted with velvet draperies and satin bedclothes. The draperies were obviously old and worn, but they were clean. The room, too, from the polished windowsills to the brick hearth, was spotless. And his few belongings had been taken from the phaeton and hung in the wardrobe. Although there seemed to be an insufficiency of household help, it was clear that someone had carefully prepared this room for him.

Despite the decaying luxury of the room, it felt like a prison to him. *What am I to do cooped up in here?* he asked himself. *And how long will this blasted storm last?* As he stared out at the snow-misted expanse spread out below him, he wondered how he could pass the time. There might be a billiard room somewhere downstairs, he supposed, where he could while away a few hours. And there was the library. He didn't think there could be any objection to his borrowing a book. But what bothered him most at this moment was simply that he was hungry. He hadn't eaten anything all day, and the cup of tea he'd had downstairs could scarcely be called a meal. A glance at his pocket watch told him it was past seven. Would it be presumptuous for an uninvited house guest to request some sustenance?

Just as the question occurred to him, there was a tap at the door. He opened it to find McTavish standing there. The bent old fellow's chest was heaving from his climb up to the tower. "Miss Livy sent me," he said between short breaths, "to request that ye join her for dinner."

"Thank you. That is most kind of her." George, though more than eager to dine, was uncertain of the requirements of dining in this household. "I'd be happy to accept," he told the butler, "but I'm afraid I have no dinner clothes with me."

"We dinna stand on ceremony here, m'lord," the butler assured him. "We're always informal. Dressin' fer dinner ain't necessary. If ye'll follow me . . ."

The butler led him down to a small room that had probably been intended as a morning room but was more than sufficient as a dining room for a small group. George noted that the round table in the center of the room was set for two. Livy was standing at the fireplace looking down at the flames, but she turned at once when McTavish announced him. "George!" she said with a small smile and held out her hand.

George studied her as he raised her hand to his lips. She was pale, and dark circles underlined her eyes. That irritating widow's cap still covered all her hair, and she still wore the muslin dress she'd had on all during the trip. She looked strained. "Livy, my dear," he said in a tone of sincere sympathy, "you look exhausted. Are you all right?"

"Yes, thank you, I'm fine. I'm only sorry that after all you've done for me I haven't been available to welcome you properly. I hope you've been made comfortable."

"Yes, Mr. McTavish has taken good care of me. How does your uncle go on?"

Her smile faded. "He suffered a very minor stroke, but he does well enough."

"Hmmph," came from the butler.

George turned to him, eyebrows raised curiously. "What did you say?"

McTavish threw a glance at Livy, who was frowning at him, but he chose to ignore the warning in her eyes. "The doctor says there be naught wrong with 'im," he told George flatly.

"You may go, McTavish," Livy ordered coldly. "Mrs. Nicol will serve us."

The butler shrugged. "What's true is true," he muttered as he shuffled out of the room. "Yer uncle's never as sick as he pretends."

The door closed behind him. "I'm so sorry," Livy said, motioning George to a seat at the table. "McTavish has too free a tongue, but chastising him has no effect. He's been with the family too long."

"But is what he said true? Is your uncle a malingerer?" George asked bluntly.

She sat down opposite him. "He's an old man," she said, lowering her eyes, "and has suffered some sort of attack. The doctor finds nothing wrong, but I notice that his mouth is a bit twisted and he can't get out of bed."

"Do you bear the burden of his care all alone?"

"No, of course not," she said hastily. "We have servants . . ."

"Nursemaids, perhaps?" he prodded.

She flicked a quick look at him. "There's Mrs. Nicol. And his man, Peters."

"No one else? If he can't get out of bed, he must need constant care."

"He doesn't like strangers about him." She reached for a wine bottle in the center of the table. "This is a fine old Madeira. May I pour you a glass?"

Her hand trembled as she poured. The poor creature had probably been caring for her uncle every moment since their arrival. But judging from her annoyance at her butler's behavior, she obviously didn't wish to talk about her uncle. He took the wineglass from her and raised it. "To better days," he said, smiling across at her.

"To better days," she echoed, smiling back.

Mrs. Nicol entered with a soup tureen. She was a stout woman with neatly bound white hair and kind eyes, but her expression was sour. " 'Tis only cabbage soup," she announced without preamble. "I wasn't prepared for company."

"I suppose cabbage soup will have to do," Livy said, but it was plain that she was not pleased.

"Cabbage soup is quite a favorite of mine," George assured them both.

Mrs. Nicol glanced at George, her expression softening. Livy's did not. "I hope, Mrs. Nicol, that you've not changed the menu for the main course," she said pointedly. "We are having the salmon, I trust."

"Yes, miss. Just because I didn't have enough beef for the barley soup you wanted doesn't mean I won't have what you want for the rest of the dinner. I'll be serving the salmon in butter sauce, just as you wished."

The housekeeper's stiff-necked petulance made Livy wince. Mrs. Nicol, pretending to be oblivious to her mistress's embarrassment, calmly spooned out the soup and departed.

George met Livy's eye and grinned at her. "She's been with the family a long time, too, I assume."

Livy blushed. "All of the staff are too familiar," she admitted. "I'm sure that after all those days at your sister's well-run household, you must be finding this a disreputable place indeed."

"Not at all. I find it generously forgiving to an unexpected intruder who was forced upon it at a time when understaffing and illness were making things difficult enough to handle."

"What a considerate response!" she exclaimed, peering across the table at him in surprise. "Can it possibly be, your lordship, that I've been somewhat misjudging you?"

"Can it, indeed?" He looked across at her in amused expectancy. "Misjudging my being autocratic and presumptuous?"

She did not laugh or respond with the expected "yes."

"Not exactly," she answered with a bewildered honesty. "I was so sure I had accurately gauged your character. I still think you autocratic and presumptuous. But several times today you've behaved in a way that seemed inconsistent with what I believe is your true character."

"Inconsistent?"

"Yes." She took a sip of her wine, and asked, in an abrupt change of subject, "How do you like the Madeira?"

But he did not want to change the subject. "How was I inconsistent?" he prodded.

She put down her glass. "You needn't make too much of this, George. I only meant that you acted in a manner other than what I expected."

"Other? In what way?"

With a sigh, she surrendered to his prodding. "Much more . . . more . . ." She seemed to be searching for an appropriate word.

"Charming?" he offered. "Winning? Adorable?"

She ignored his assistance. "Kind," she said.

"Kind?" He reared back in his seat in mock offense. "After building my hopes up to expect something flattering, you offer *kind*?"

She shrugged. "That's the best I can do. Now let's stop this nonsense. Eat your soup."

He did as she asked, but he had no wish to stop probing into her analysis of his character. If nothing else, it was pleasing banter. "I don't see how being kind is inconsistent with your assessment of my character, ma'am. Even if you find me riddled with bad qualities, can't I have a few good ones without being inconsistent?"

"No. Being kind doesn't fit with being . . ." She searched again for a word.

He offered help again. "Obnoxious? Bullying? Irksome?"

"Yes. And let's not forget authoritative and presumptuous."

"Good God! All of that?" he asked in pretended dismay, but inside the dismay was real. He wasn't as amused as he pretended. How much of this teasing description, he wondered, did she really believe?

There was a long moment of silence. Then he said quietly, "If all that is true, I can understand why kindness doesn't fit the picture."

"It certainly doesn't," she agreed, her tone still bantering, "therefore, the most logical explanation must be that either your acts of kindness are insincere, or my assessment of you is askew."

Those words gave him a feeling of relief. "Since I'm not at all *aware* of any acts of kindness," he said with a smile, "they can't possibly be insincere. So you'd better begin revising your assessment."

She returned his smile. "Perhaps I should."

They finished their soups in an atmosphere of contented companionship. But when he put down his spoon, he studied her with a sudden puzzled frown. "I think, Livy, that your character, too, is inconsistent."

She looked up across at him with eyebrows raised. "How so?"

"It's your changeable moods. At times like this, you are so easy to—"

This interesting beginning was interrupted by the abrupt entrance of Mrs. Nicol bearing the salmon. "Here it is, nice and hot," she announced, showing the steaming platter to her mistress. "And McTavish is right behind me with those little carrots you like and a bowl of mushrooms Provençale."

On cue, McTavish appeared in the doorway. But just as he was about to step over the threshold, there was a shout from somewhere nearby. It was so loud it seemed to shake the window glass. *"Livy! Where the blazes are ye?"*

Livy looked stricken.

Mrs. Nicol rolled her eyes heavenward and muttered, "Oh, no!"

"There! Y' see?" sighed the butler as he set down the bowls and hurried out.

"I'm sorry, George," Livy said hurriedly. She jumped to her feet and headed toward the door, adding to the housekeeper, "Finish serving his lordship," over her shoulder as she ran out.

"But what about you?" the housekeeper cried after her. "You haven't had a proper morsel all day!"

But Livy was gone. Mrs. Nicol sighed, shrugged, and turned to serve George his dinner. "That man won't let her live," she muttered as she shoveled a helping of salmon onto his plate.

George, stricken by the sudden change in atmosphere, sat gaping at the open doorway. "Is there anything I can do?" he asked the housekeeper.

"I wish there were," Mrs. Nicol said sadly, spooning a large helping of savory mushrooms on his plate. "But please, your lordship, eat your dinner. Miss Olivia's been worrying about you all day. She'd be mighty unhappy if you went hungry."

George looked down at his plate that was laden with delicious food. A few moments ago he would have devoured it all, every morsel, with greedy enthusiasm. But now, suddenly, he was no longer hungry. His appetite had completely deserted him.

Eighteen

Sitting there alone at the dining table, George was discomfitted by everything that was spread before his eyes: Livy's empty plate, the platter in the center of the table on which Livy's rapidly cooling portion of salmon lay, and her wineglass, still half full. A bowl of cabbage soup and half a glass of wine had been all she'd had to eat. That could scarcely be considered adequate nourishment. It was deucedly unfair that she'd not been given time to finish her dinner.

A wave of righteous indignation swept over him. He could not permit such injustice to be ignored. If he had any manhood left, he would find Sir Andrew, Livy's curmudgeonly uncle, and give him a piece of his mind. *What sort of fellow would I be if I did nothing?* he asked himself. In answer, he jumped to his feet, placed Livy's empty plate over the salmon to keep it as warm as possible, and stalked out of the room.

It did not take long to find Sir Andrew's room. The sounds of raised voices led him to a closed door at the top of the wide main staircase. As he paused for a moment to gird his loins, he heard a hoarse voice shout, "Do ye ca' this watery concoction gruel? It reeks o' leeks! Didna I tell ye plainly, no leeks?"

Then a female voice said, "But there aren't any—"

"Stick yer maw, woman!" the hoarse-voiced man shouted. "Do ye think me so far gone I dinna ken leeks when I smell 'em?"

"Please, Uncle," came Livy's voice, "you know that Mrs. Nicol would never—"

"Blast ye, must I endure a callieshangle at every turn?" came the loudest shout of all, followed by the crackling sound of crockery being thrown against something hard.

George squared his shoulders, knocked firmly, and not waiting for a reply, threw the door open.

One quick glance took it all in. It was like the setting of a play, with all the actors frozen in place. Against the rear wall was a large, canopied bed, its drapes tied back so that the central player in the drama—the white-lipped, white-haired, large-nosed Sir Andrew—was clearly seen. At his left a lanky, ruddy-cheeked fellow (probably Peters, the valet) was bending over him in the act of dabbing at his mouth with a towel. Livy, the heroine of the drama, was standing at her uncle's right, trying to urge him back against the pile of pillows. On the floor near the right wall, Mrs. Nicol was kneeling down, picking up pieces of broken crockery. And, standing just behind her, McTavish was wiping drippings of pasty gruel from the wall. At this moment, however, all the action had stopped as the players gaped at the intruder poised in the doorway.

Sir Andrew was the first to speak. "Who the devil may *ye* be?" he snarled.

"George Frobisher, sir," George said with a bow.

"It's Lord Chadleigh, Uncle," Livy said hastily. "He's the gentleman who took me home from Yorkshire."

"So that's the wanwyt, is it?" Sir Andrew growled, throwing off her restraining arm and glowering at the newcomer. "Ye're the one who connived t' seduce my niece into spending last night at an inn with ye!"

"Uncle!" Livy cried, horrified.

George was startled into a laugh. "If you think, sir, that I can 'connive' up a snowstorm in order to facilitate a seduction, you greatly overestimate my powers."

McTavish snickered, earning him a furious glare from his employer.

But Sir Andrew was not easily distracted from the main object of his venom. He turned his glare back to George. "And what, may I ask," he barked, "are ye doin' here?"

"I've invited him to stay while the storm lasts," Livy explained.

"Aye, aye, that I ken," her uncle snapped. "I didna wish fer ye t' put him out in the snow. What I'm askin' is what he's doing *here* . . . in this room!"

"I came to remind Miss Henshaw that her salmon is getting cold," George said with bland nonchalance.

"Her *what*?"

Livy threw George a glance of reproof. "It's nothing, Uncle," she said. "Nothing at all."

"Her salmon," George repeated, ignoring her. "It's getting cold."

"Is that so?" Sir Andrew asked, his white eyebrows knitting together.

"Yes, sir, quite so. And that's too bad, you know, since I'm told that this dinner is the only opportunity she's had to eat all day."

Sir Andrew turned his glare to his niece. "Ye should've *told* me ye didna finish yer dinner," he shouted. "Take yerself off at once and finish it!"

Livy, drawing in a breath as if to restrain her feelings of anger, shook her head. "You haven't had your meal yet, Uncle. I can eat after we've fixed you a nice, thick oatmeal broth with those bits of lamb you like so much."

"Nae, nae, Mrs. Nicol can take care o' me," her uncle declared, less loudly but just as firmly. "Go along, woman, go along." And he waved her away.

George followed Livy out of the sickroom, feeling triumphant. He'd behaved like a white knight and rescued the maiden from servitude and starvation. She would surely fall upon him in tearful gratitude the moment that they were alone.

As soon as he closed the door behind him, however, she wheeled on him in fury. "How dared you!" she cried, her voice shaking.

"What?" He could only blink in utter confusion.

"Of all the damnable presumption! How dared you to take it upon yourself to interfere with the running of this household?"

"Interfere?" The accusation made no sense to him. "In what way did I—?"

"After being here less than a day, you cannot know how things are managed here. Yet you barged into my uncle's room without being asked and proceeded to manipulate matters that you know nothing about."

George was astounded. "But I only wanted to free you to have your dinner."

"You think you were being kind, no doubt."

"Well . . . yes."

"Not authoritative and presumptuous?"

"Not at all."

She put her hands on her hips in a stance of disgusted superiority. "Then let me tell you, my lord, that you're off the mark. To try to free me from the sickroom was, without a doubt, an act of presumption."

"I don't see—"

"Of course you don't see. The fact is that I *wanted* to be there. I try to be present at my uncle's bedside as much as possible, for very good reasons."

"Why?" George asked, trying his best to understand. "The man is obviously not at death's door. You yourself told me that the doctor could find nothing wrong with him. So why must you hover over him all day?"

"The why of it is not your concern. But in my own defense, I will explain this much: if I left him alone with the servants, he might become so abusive that they would leave his employ. We've lost too many already. So I stay there as a buffer against his bile. As long as they're convinced I'm on their side, they are willing to endure him."

"Oh." George, nonplussed, still couldn't understand. Nor could he feel any sympathy for her. The situation she'd described seemed to him to be ludicrous in the extreme. A spoiled, hot-tempered, foolish old man was tyrannizing the entire household. How, he wondered, could a strong-minded, sensible woman like Olivia Henshaw permit such a state to continue? But it was not his place to point that out. An uninvited guest had no right to comment on what he was not meant to see. "I'm sorry," he murmured, not knowing what else to say.

"Saying 'sorry' is easy. Mending matters is not."

"Is there anything I can do to mend them?"

"No. The best you can do is go up to bed."

"Very well, then, ma'am, I will." Since he'd been so summarily dismissed, he turned at once to the stairs. "I bid you good night."

She didn't need to recognize the stiffness in his posture to know she'd offended him. "My lord?" she called after him, her voice just a bit conciliatory.

Keeping his hand on the banister, he turned only his head. "Yes?"

She looked down at the toe of her shoe that was making nervous little circles on the carpet. "I was rude. I didn't mean to . . . it's just . . ." She looked up and met his eye. "I know you meant to be kind."

"Yes, I did." He ventured a small, wry smile. "I thought I was being a white knight rescuing a maiden in distress."

But at those seemingly innocent words, she again became furious. "That's just it!" she exclaimed, clenching her fists and stamping her foot. "That's exactly what makes me wild."

"I don't understand. *What* makes you wild?"

"Your . . . your . . . your blasted smug attitude! You treat me as you would a helpless, befuddled old maiden aunt. I am *not* helpless. Dash it, George Frobisher, I don't want or need your help, your sympathy, your white-knight kindness! I am *not your little old maiden aunt!*"

George was taken aback. "I never . . . I don't . . ."

"Oh, never mind," she said, throwing up her hands in

disgust. It occurred to him that her disgust was directed as much toward herself as to him. As she stalked off, she added, "Just . . . just . . ."

"Yes?"

She didn't bother to look back. "Just . . . *go to bed!*"

Nineteen

The bed with its velvet hangings was comfortable enough, but George found it difficult to fall asleep. He tossed about for what seemed like hours. Livy's angry accusation kept nagging at him. What had she meant when she'd said that he treated her like a maiden aunt? He didn't understand exactly what she was accusing him of. *How does one behave toward a maiden aunt?* he asked himself. After all, he'd never had one. He suspected that one would be polite and respectful toward a maiden aunt. If that was how he'd been treating Livy—and he certainly hoped he had!—was there something wrong with that? Shouldn't all ladies be treated courteously and respectfully? Unless he'd overdone it. Was Livy finding him too polite? Too formal? Too . . . too . . . ?

A sudden noise startled him awake. He sat up abruptly and rubbed his eyes, surprised to realize that he'd managed to fall asleep after all. But what was the dreadful sound that had awakened him?

It took him a moment to shake off the cobwebs of sleep before he remembered where he was. He had no idea of the time, but it was certainly not morning. The room was shrouded in darkness and no evidence of morning light seeped in from the many windows. Yet he could hear the sounds of querulous voices and running feet. Curious, he got out of bed and went to the door. As he opened it, he heard a woman cry, quite distinctly, "Get me some bandages, quick!"

The words were alarming. Something terrible must have happened. He had to go and offer help, although he suspected that Livy might not wish for his presence at whatever crisis was now occurring. She would undoubtedly find him presumptuous and interfering. She always seemed to find him so. He wondered, as he lit a candle, why she always found fault with him. He'd often been told by friends and acquaintances that he was a good sort of fellow. Why did she dislike him so?

Nevertheless, the sounds of urgent voices and running feet made him decide to act at once. Barefoot, and in his nightshirt, he ran out of the room and made his way downstairs. In the hallway of the floor below his, a dim ray of candlelight led him to the head of the main stairway in front of Sir Andrew's bedroom. There he discovered the source of the light. It had come from a candelabra that had been placed on the floor, lighting two figures seated on the top step. As George came closer, he recognized Livy and Mrs. Nicol. They were both in their nightclothes, Livy bent over, with her head lowered onto her knees, and Mrs. Nicol holding her about the shoulders. George came up behind them. "Is something amiss?" he asked.

They both turned. At his first glance, George drew in a gasping breath. What he saw made him speechless. Livy had been hurt. Her long hair, unbound and falling wildly about her face and shoulders, was restricted at the top by a wide bandage that was wound about her head like a tilted hat, dipping low on her forehead just above her left eye. A smear of blood was already seeping through the bandage, marking with frightening accuracy the place on her forehead where she'd evidently been wounded. "Good God!" he muttered when his voice returned. "What happened?"

"Sir Andrew is what happened," came McTavish's voice from just behind him. The butler came round to the seated women and handed Livy a cup of steaming tea. "He threw a lamp at her."

"He threw a lamp, but not at me," Livy said in a quiet voice. "It was an accident."

"Hummph," grunted the butler.

George sat down beside her. "Are you in pain?"

"A bit," she said, "but I'll be all right."

"You'll have a black eye and a scar," Mrs. Nicol declared sourly.

"Both of which will go away in time." Livy lifted her head. "Don't raise a dust over this, Mrs. Nicol," she said, trying to sound firm despite a noticeable tremor in her voice. "Thank you for tending to me. Now, please, go off to bed, all of you."

"And what about you, miss?" the butler wanted to know. "You ain't going back in there to see yer uncle again, are ye?"

"No. The dose of laudanum Peters gave him should keep him sleeping 'til tomorrow. I'll just finish my tea, and then I'll go to bed, too."

Mrs. Nicol got to her feet, and the two servants each took a candle from the candelabra and reluctantly started down the hall toward the back stairs. George followed them until they were out of Livy's hearing. Then he caught their arms to hold them back. "What brought on this latest burst of temper?" he demanded to know. "Did the old fellow smell leeks in his gruel again?"

Mrs. Nicol snorted. "So you heard that, did you? Well, this time, it was a stomach spasm."

"He woke up in some pain," the butler said, "an' he rang for Peters—"

"—not caring a bit that it wasn't quite four in the morning," the housekeeper put in.

"Peters came running," the butler continued, "an' found him standing up, bent over and yowling like he had a knife in his innards. Poor Peters was scared out of 'is wits."

"So he ran for me," Mrs. Nicol went on. "Miss Henshaw's room is right down the hall, and she heard the commotion. So did Bridie, of course. They both came running into Sir Andrew's room, and the three of us got him into bed. Whatever it was that bothered him seemed to have eased, but Miss Henshaw asked Peters to hold the lamp over him so she could see his face properly."

"To see if 'e looked like 'e had the apoplexy, ye know," McTavish explained.

"When Peters held up the lamp," the housekeeper went on, "a bit of hot oil must have dripped on his face. You'd think a little bit of a burn wouldn't cause such a foofaraw, but Sir Andrew let out a yowl you could hear all the way to Edinburgh."

"That's probably what woke me," George said.

"It woke me, that's fer certain," the butler said. "I came runnin' in my nightshirt, just like you."

"Anyway," Mrs. Nicol went on, "His High and Mighty grabbed the lamp from Peters's hand and flung it away, not looking to see where. It hit Miss Henshaw right on the head. The poor lady dropped down like a stone."

"That's when I come in," the butler continued. "It was a feery-fary, it was! On one side, Peters was tryin' to quiet Sir Andrew. On the other, Mrs. Nicol was cradlin' Miss Henshaw's head an' cryin', an' Bridie was havin' hysterics. So, first I ordered Bridie off to bed. Then Mrs. Nicol an' I picked up Miss Olivia an' brought 'er round. When she came to, she insisted that she was fine, but we saw her forehead trickling blood, so, while Peters gave the old man a dose of laudanum, I ran for the bandages. The rest ye know."

"Yes," George said with a troubled frown. "Well, thank you both."

He bid them good night and returned to where Livy was sitting, drinking her tea. When he sat down beside her, she put down the cup and looked at him. "I'm sorry your sleep was disturbed, George. Please don't worry about this. I'll be fine. Do go back to bed."

"I will, when you do. Meanwhile, with your permission, I'd like to tighten your bandage. The blood seems to be seeping down into your eye."

"Thank you," she said, turning her face up to him. "That is kind of you."

"Kind? Not presumptuous?"

She smiled weakly. "Not this time."

With the skill he'd learned in Spain in dealing with wounds, he undid the bandage, and studied the cut on her forehead. Relieved to see it was not as extensive as he feared, he mopped up the blood with the sleeve of his nightshirt, smoothed out her hair, and began the process of rewinding. "Does this sort of accident happen often?" he asked as he worked.

"No, of course not," she said. "My uncle is really . . . that is, he is usually . . . very k—"

"You were not going to say 'kind,' were you?" he asked with a scornful laugh.

She tried to laugh with him, but her shoulders began to shake, and the laugh became a hiccough, and the hiccough became a sob. "He is n-not well, you see. N-not at all w-w—" Suddenly she was overcome with chest-heaving sobs.

Instinctively, he put his arms about her. "That's all right," he said, patting her shoulder. "You don't have to make excuses for him. Not to me."

"You d-don't understand," she said, weeping into his shoulder. "He t-t-took m-me in when I was s-s-small and n-n-nobody else w-w-wanted me."

"It's all right," he said soothingly. "Don't cry."

But she kept on sobbing. It was as if a wellspring of tears, which she'd held back for a very long time, suddenly burst forth. And in the midst of the wracking sobs, some almost-incoherent words came bubbling out of her. She seemed compelled to explain to George her uncle's part in her life. George managed to grasp that her mother had died at her birth, that her father had contracted diphtheria and died when she was eight, that her uncle had taken her in but had never been capable of showing her much affection. It was indeed a pathetic story.

George didn't know how to comfort her. All he could do was say "There, there," and rock her gently back and forth in his arms.

It was strange, holding her this way. Through her thin nightdress, he could feel the womanliness of her, the softness that he hadn't been able to see when she was fully clothed. Holding her so closely, he felt moved in a way he'd never felt holding a woman. It was as if she filled an empty place in him, a vacuum he didn't know was there. As the trembling sobs decreased, he knew she would soon be withdrawing from his embrace. Astonishingly, he didn't want that to happen. He didn't feel ready to let her go.

But she didn't withdraw. When at last her weeping subsided, she lifted a hand to her cheeks and, blushing, wiped the wetness away. "I d-don't know what came over me," she said, peeping up at him, her voice still thick. "I seem to be behaving just the way I dislike . . . indeed, quite like a maiden aunt."

"Not to me," he said, and lifted her chin. Her eyes were still wet and red-rimmed and her mouth was swollen from the flood of tears. The sight of her face startled him. In spite of the red-rimmed eyes and the ridiculous bandage over her forehead, that face seemed lovely. How could he ever have thought of it as plain and spinsterish? It was as if he'd been blind, and his sight was suddenly restored.

He could not resist the impulse. He leaned down to that lovely face and pressed those swollen lips to his.

For a long, delicious moment, she did not resist him. In fact she seemed to raise herself up against him so that her breasts pressed against his chest. That little movement sent a lightning jolt through his entire body, reminding him of what he'd felt when he'd glimpsed his Venus all those years ago. Then she stiffened, pushed him away, and stared at him, eyes wide with shock. He, too, was shocked. It was disconcerting, this feeling like a seventeen-year-old.

A distant clock struck five, bringing him back to the

here-and-now. Bemused by his own feelings, he did not notice that the shock in her eyes had turned to fury. He grinned at her. "You can't call *that* treating you like my maiden aunt."

"No," she said icily, getting to her feet. "I call it unforgivable."

The tone of her voice was worse than a slap. It struck him like a douse of cold water. "Unforgivable?" he asked in disbelief.

She looked down at him with what he thought was loathing. "I don't know why I ever found you kind," she said. "When it really matters, you are quite heartless." And, pulling her nightdress tightly around her as if for protection, she ran away down the corridor and out of his sight.

Twenty

When George returned to his room, he discovered that the fire had died. It was no surprise; what else could he expect in this ill-run household? The room was so icy cold that his breath made a cloud in the air. And after having puttered about the hallways in his bare feet, he was sure his toes were frozen. But all these ills were insignificant when compared to the pain of Livy's vituperative reaction to his kiss. His usual cheerful spirit had received a severe blow, making him wish more than ever that he'd never embarked on this damnable journey. "Blast Felicia for urging it," he cursed aloud, "and blast me for giving in to her!"

He wrapped himself up in all the bedclothes he could find and threw himself down on the bed. Mercifully, he fell asleep almost at once. But it seemed only a moment later that he was being shaken awake. He opened his eyes to find Timmy bending over him. "Sorry to wake ye, m'lord," the boy said, "but ye did say ye wanted to leave 'ere as soon as we could. It stopped snowin' last night."

"What time is it?" George asked thickly.

"Almost seven. I made up the fire, an' I didn't wake ye 'til the room was warm enough fer ye to dress."

George groaned. His tongue was stuck to the roof of his mouth. He could hardly manage a thank you to his eager tiger. He'd had less than two hours of sleep since his encounter with Livy on the stairway. His body seemed to cry out for more sleep, but he fought the urge and untangled himself from his cocoon of bedclothes. In an act of true courage, he got out of bed and padded over to one of the windows. When he opened the draperies, he discovered a world gleaming in brilliant sunshine. Snow, at least a foot deep, covered the landscape like a soft comforter, sparkling white and unmarked by human imprints. The view, though unquestionably lovely, depressed him, for it did not look promising for travel. George wanted nothing so much as to take his leave, especially after Livy's cold rejection a few hours ago, but from what he could see below the roads would be impassable. "We'd never make it through the drifts," he told Timmy glumly.

But Timmy didn't agree. "Yes, we can, m'lord," he chortled. "Mr. Shotton, the coachman, tole me he could take off the wheels of the phaeton and put on a pair of runners—like a sleigh."

"A sleigh?" George's eyes widened. "He can convert the phaeton to a sleigh? What a wonderful idea!" The possibility that they might be able to depart was as intoxicating to him as a drink of aged port. "How long do you suppose it would take him to do the job?"

"Don't know, m'lord, but I'll get 'im right on it. After all, he don't 'ave anythin' else to do, whut wi' the roads closed."

"Good man!" George clapped him on the back, considerably cheered. After all, it was Monday. If they could start today, he might still make it back to London in time for the ball. "Give him all the help you can, Timmy, and if the two of you can get us ready to leave by noon, there'll be a handsome vail for each of you."

Later, dressed and ravenously hungry, he went down from his tower room to see if he could find McTavish. He had not yet determined how meals were provided in this peculiar household, but if he found no breakfast laid out in the morning room, he intended to coax the butler to provide him—and promptly, too!—with something edible.

As he approached the morning-room door, he heard voices from within. He paused, not wishing to intrude. But neither did he wish to lose an opportunity to eat. While he hesitated, he heard Livy's voice. "But, Dr. Evans," she was saying, "he was doubled over in pain."

"That may be," a man's voice replied, "but I could not detect any sign of abdominal distress. Nor any other symptom of illness. It's the same as the past half-dozen times I've examined him. I can find nothing wrong."

"I can't understand it," she said, her voice full of concern. "There must be *something* . . ."

"It could be merely imaginary," the doctor said.

"Imaginary?"

The doorknob turned, and the door opened. George, embarrassed at the prospect of being caught eaves-dropping, stepped back out of the way. The doctor—a short, stocky man with a ring of gray hair circling an otherwise bald head and a pair of formidable eyebrows over bright, shrewd eyes—came out of the room, shrugging himself into a heavy overcoat. "Yes, my dear," he was saying over his shoulder to Livy, who was following him, "there are many who suffer from imaginary illnesses."

"But is it safe to merely *assume* his pains are not real?" she asked.

"I feel quite sure, in this case. He suggested to me that his symptoms might be caused by stomach gout. The term 'stomach gout' hasn't been used for fifty years. He probably heard the words from his father. Since no one ever quite knew what the symptoms of stomach gout were, I think it's safe to assume he's imagining the disease. Much as he imagined in the past that he suffered from putrified blood, fatal consumption, and dropsy."

At this point, Livy noticed George standing against the wall. "Oh," she said, her expression changing from worry to surprise to awkward stiffness. "My lord . . . er . . . good morning."

"Good morning, ma'am," George answered with equal awkwardness.

Livy turned to the doctor. "Dr. Evans, this is our . . . our house guest, Lord Chadleigh. My lord, this is our physician, the good Dr. Evans."

"How do you do?" George put out his hand. "You must be a good doctor indeed, to come out in all this snow. How did you manage it?"

The doctor looked with interest from George to Livy and back again. Then, with a wide smile, he shook George's hand heartily. "A pleasure to meet you, my lord," he said. "I came on horseback. My old nag is accustomed to picking her way through snowdrifts."

"I hope my horses will do as well," George remarked.

The doctor's heavy brows rose in surprise. "You don't mean to leave today, do you?"

"I'm afraid I do. I'm expected back in London the day after tomorrow."

The doctor, who'd been in the act of pulling a fur hat down over his ears, froze for a moment and threw Livy a look of disappointment. Then he shook his head. "You'd have to do some miraculous driving to make it," he muttered to George as he turned to leave. "It's a three-day trip."

"Not if you don't stop to sleep," George said.

As he watched Livy walk away to lead Dr. Evans down to the outer doorway, George wondered why the doctor seemed disappointed at his announcement of his intention to depart. Had the fellow had hopes of some sort of liaison between himself and Livy, hopes that were dashed by his intention to return to London? The good doctor must be fond of Livy, George thought, to show such concern for her personal affairs. But then, everyone, it seemed, was fond of Livy—his sister, the stuffy Horace Thomsett, all the servants in this grim household, and everyone else who . . .

McTavish appeared at that moment and led him into the morning room. To his relief, he discovered that a generous breakfast buffet was already laid out. While the butler was loading his plate, George's thoughts turned to what he'd overheard the doctor saying about Sir Andrew.

Perhaps the butler could answer some questions that had been troubling him. "I was wondering, McTavish," he said casually, "if you know why Sir Andrew can't walk."

"Who says he can't?" the butler hooted. "He can walk, out a doot! Peters an' me, we once proved he can."

"Oh?" George's eyebrows rose. "How did you do that?"

McTavish grinned mischievously. "We put a dose of Joanna's powder in his tea."

"Joanna's powder?"

" 'Tis a vile concoction of Alicante soap, mercury, and snails. It stirs up the innards, y' see. In only five minutes, it worked on him." The butler's grin widened at the recollection. "Ye should've seen him jump up and dash for the chamber pot."

George could hardly contain a guffaw. "Then you believe he really can walk?"

"Fer certain. When he has a mind to." McTavish set a plate of York ham and buttered eggs before him and then heaved a resigned sigh. "And now I'm off to serve him his breakfast. If I'm in luck, he winna throw it at me."

George was not alone long. A few moments later, Livy returned and, glancing at what McTavish had put on George's plate, went to the buffet. She set a scone on a small plate and spread some jam on it. Then she poured him a cup of tea. Without speaking a word to him, she placed the scone and the tea on the table before him. George threw her a quizzical look. "Do you intend never to speak to me again?" he asked.

"I shall say whatever is necessary," she answered flatly.

"Will you bid me good-bye when the carriage is ready?"

"Oh?" She seemed surprised. "Then you do intend to leave today?"

"Yes, I do. So, ma'am, will you wish me godspeed?"

"Of course. I haven't forgotten my manners." She turned away and lowered her head. "But, my lord," she said as if forcing the words out, "in spite of whatever has passed between us, I hope you understand that you are welcome to take refuge under this roof for as long as necessary. There is no need for you to battle these snowy roads unnecessarily. I did not—I do not—intend to banish you from the premises."

"I never thought you would," he said, taking a bite of ham. "But, as you know, I promised my friend to be back in London by the day after tomorrow. Therefore I shall be taking my leave this afternoon."

She nodded. "Then I wish you a safe journey."

"Thank you." He looked up at her. "Will you sit down and join me for breakfast? There is something I'd like to say to you before I go."

At those words, her head came up abruptly, and she swung around to face him. "If you intend to apologize for last night," she snapped, "then you may as well save your breath. I have no intention of forgiving you. Ever."

"I have no intention of apologizing," he said calmly. "I wish to speak of another matter entirely."

"Oh." Taken aback, she stood motionless for a moment. Then she drew in a breath of surrender. "In that case, I *will* join you for breakfast." She went to the buffet, took a scone and a cup of tea, and went back to the table. When she'd seated herself, she looked across at him. "Well?"

"I heard what the doctor said about Sir Andrew. About his imagining all those illnesses."

"Yes?"

"I don't think they're imaginary at all. I think your uncle concocts them quite knowingly. For a specific purpose."

Livy stiffened. "I don't know what you mean," she said carefully, lifting a cup to her lips to avoid his eyes.

"I think you do. Look me in the eye, my dear, and tell me honestly that you don't know what I mean."

"I don't," she insisted.

"I mean, ma'am, that these pretended illnesses are the means by which Sir Andrew rules this house, and you know it." He put down his fork and leaned across the table toward her. "What I can't understand, Livy, is how a woman as strong-willed and intelligent as you can let yourself be manipulated so."

"There you go again!" Slamming down her cup, Livy jumped to her feet, her lips trembling in a rage. "Is there *anything* that can stop your arrogant interference in things you know nothing about?"

"But I do know about this! You told me yourself." He stood up and started round the table toward her. "I know you're grateful for his making you his ward. But don't you see that he's taking a terribly unfair advantage of that gratitude?"

White-lipped, she put up her hand to stop his advance. "You've said quite enough! None of these matters are your concern. Since you shall be leaving today, you can put them out of your mind, as I shall put your offensive behavior out of mine. Thank goodness we need never face each other again! Good-bye, my lord, and since you asked for it, I wish you godspeed." And with those angry words echoing in the air like the distant rumble of thunder, she stalked out of the room.

Twenty-One

George sat slumped on the rear seat of the phaeton, feeling miserable. He could hear Timmy, up on the box outside, whistling cheerfully as the carriage glided over the snow on its new runners. He knew he, too, should be cheerful, for with any luck they would make it to London in time to dress for the ball. But he couldn't seem to thrust off the cloud of depression that surrounded him like a cloak. It was not Livy's unkind goodbye alone that nagged at him, although that itself was enough to wound a fellow's spirit. After all, it was not pleasant to be called an interfering, arrogant meddler. And then there was her scathing response to his kiss. She'd interpreted a sincere, affectionate embrace as an act of cruelty. He would never understand her! But it was more than those insults that troubled him. It was Livy herself—the dreadful life she lived that she would do nothing to improve. Why did she not see how her uncle was exploiting her?

Of course, he could not deny that her numerous blows to his self-image had cut him deeply. In all his twenty-seven years, he could not remember anyone who'd taken him in such complete dislike. True, the start of their association had been his own fault—the disappointed look on his face when he'd first seen her must have been more damaging to her than he'd believed. But he'd tried in every way to erase that first impression. She'd reacted negatively to his every attempt to undo it. *I don't want your kindness,* she'd told him over and over. He found that repeated rejection bewildering. What else could she have wanted from him? Damnation, he would never understand her!

His mind kept returning to the moment when she'd cried out her story in his arms. He'd responded with a sympathetic embrace. (It *was* a sympathetic embrace, wasn't it?) Why had she interpreted that kiss as heartless? How could an act of warm sympathy be heartless? No, no, no, he would never understand her!

To be honest, he had to admit that on his part the kiss had been more than sympathetic. He'd felt a surprisingly strong physical desire for her. Could she have sensed that? Did she find such physical intimacy abhorrent? Was she a prude? Until this moment, he'd forgotten that she'd seemed like a dried-up old maid when he'd first glimpsed her. She did not seem so now, but perhaps his first impression wasn't far off. Her behavior after the kiss could be called puritanical, couldn't it? Was she a straitlaced spinster after all?

But since he would never understand her, there was no point in gnawing away at these questions. There was nothing for him to do but put the whole experience behind him. *Leave her to her deuced, self-imposed fate,* he told himself. As she'd informed him more than once, it was none of his concern.

Nevertheless, it irked him that no one in that benighted household had the courage to speak up to the choleric Sir Andrew. What that man needed was a good verbal clobbering. If he, George Frobisher, were any sort of man, he would have done it himself. Never mind Livy's objection, a proper man would have acted on instinct—the instinct of a true gentleman!—and given the damned curmudgeon the drubbing he deserved.

George sat up in his seat, suddenly alert. He ought to do it, he realized. It would be the right thing to do. He could still turn round, retrace his steps, and give the old bounder a piece of his mind. Was he a gentleman or wasn't he?

But he was also a man of his word, and he'd given that word to Bernard. He'd sworn he'd be back in plenty of time to take Bernard to the ball. They'd already driven four hours away from Lockerbie. If he turned back now, he'd lose eight hours, thus making it impossible to make it to London in time.

With a sigh, he leaned back on the seat again. *There is a tide in the affairs of men,* Shakespeare had written. But he'd missed the tide. By being too obedient to Livy's restrictions, he'd delayed too long. He was now forced to clench his fists, grit his teeth, and obey her stricture to mind his own affairs.

Mind my own affairs . . . mind my own affairs . . . George repeated the phrase to himself in time to the soft, rhythmic plish-plish of the horses' hooves as they picked their way through the snow. *Mind my own affairs.* But the repeated admonition became just meaningless words. What he really wanted to do, with a deepening sense of urgency, was to act like a man.

On a sudden impulse, he reached over, lowered the window, and shouted out to Timmy, "Pull up, old man! I'll take the reins. We're going back!"

With the wind in his face, he drove north again. Poor, bewildered Timmy insisted on remaining beside him on the box to keep watch over his master, convinced that his lordship had lost his mind. Pushing the horses to their utmost, George pulled up in front of Henshaw Castle in less than two hours. Then he threw the reins to Timmy. "Walk the horses for a bit," he ordered. "I won't be long." And he ran up the stone steps.

McTavish, having heard the horses, hurried on his unsteady legs into the entry hall. "My lord!" he cried in alarm. "Have ye had an accident?"

"Never mind me," George said, taking the steps of the main stairway two at a time, the capes of his greatcoat flapping. He burst into Sir Andrew's bedroom without knocking. Peters, in the act of placing a woolen shawl about Sir Andrew's shoulders, looked up in alarm. "Peters," George ordered before the two men could recover

from their shock, "take yourself off. I want to speak to
Sir Andrew alone."

The old man's face reddened in fury. "How dare ye
burst in here like this!" he roared.

"Peters, go!" George said firmly.

"But, yer lordship," the valet said, frightened, "I
can't—"

"Peters," Sir Andrew barked, "stay right here!"

George grasped the valet by his lapels and forcibly
backed him across the room and out the door. "Wait
right there," he ordered, shutting the door in Peters's
agonized face and pulling closed the bolt. "Now then,
my good sir, I have a few choice words to say to you."

"Peters," Sir Andrew shouted, "get McTavish and
Shotton and break the door down!"

"He can't hear you through that door," George said.
"I'm afraid, sir, that you're stuck with me for as long as
I choose, so be still and listen to me, or I shall have to
remove my ascot and stuff it in your mouth."

The old man made a strangled sound in his throat.

"You needn't panic," George assured him. "I mean
you no physical harm. I only want to say a few words
to you."

Relieved, Sir Andrew's high color receded. But he still
eyed George with loathing. "Ye've a good bit o' cheek,"
he muttered in sullen surrender. "What is it ye have
t' say?"

George walked to the foot of the bed and faced the
old man squarely. "I'd like to understand you, sir," he
said. "What sort of man are you? How can you lie there,
day after day, pretending to be ill and helpless, when
you know perfectly well that you're healthy as a horse?"

"I am *not*—"

George glared at him. "You are not to speak, is that
understood? Not a *word*. And yes, you *are* as healthy as
a horse. I have it from your doctor and from everyone
else who knows you. It's plain as pikestaff that you've
found this lazy, cowardly, pinch-penny way to keep control over this household. Each member of the staff has

to do the work of three, and what is worse, you use your own niece as a bond slave!"

Sir Andrew made a move to speak, but George put up a restraining hand.

"Yes," he went on, "that's what I said, bond slave! A drudge, a poor menial who works harder than the lowest kitchen maid, at your beck and call twenty-four hours a day! She accepts the role because she's full of gratitude to you for taking her in and making her your ward. But you didn't take her in out of generosity, did you? No, don't bother to answer. I know why you did it. It was just to get yourself a caring nurse at no cost to yourself!"

"That's a damned lie!" the old man burst out. "I love the child!"

"Child? You call her a child? Haven't you noticed that she's past thirty and looks even older? A fine old spinster you've made of her! And you call it *love*? It's a strange sort of love, to keep the woman enslaved and deprived of a life of her own."

Sir Andrew, his pale blue, agonized eyes fixed on George's face, emitted a low groan.

But George did not soften at the pathetic sound. "From what I can see," he declared, hoping his final words would leave a mark on the man, "you're nothing but a selfish, tightfisted curmudgeon who makes life a misery for everyone around him. I warn you, Sir Andrew, that if you don't make things better for those who depend on you while you still have *this* life, then you'll find the devil giving you a taste of your own in the *next*!"

With that, he wheeled about, unbolted the door, and stormed out of the room. Outside the door stood a nervous Peters, a grinning McTavish, and a stunned Livy. But George did not pause to acknowledge them. Without so much as a nod, he strode past them, ran down the stairway and out the door. Down on the roadway, the carriage was waiting. He leaped up on the box, took hold of the reins, and off they went.

As the phaeton-turned-sleigh slid over the snow, George began to feel foolish. He'd enjoyed every moment of that encounter, but perhaps he'd been merely self-indulgent. Now he wondered if his diatribe would do Livy any good. It was only a fusillade of words, after all. Could words change the nature of a spoiled old man?

Night had fallen. Even if they drove the whole distance without stopping, the ball would have ended by the time they reached London. Had he broken his promise to his best friend merely for the pleasure of giving Sir Andrew a piece of his mind? With a groan of shame, he dropped his head in his hands. "I'm so sorry, Bernard," he muttered aloud. "I've let you down. Forgive me."

Twenty-Two

$\mathcal{B}$ernard, waiting in London for some sign of George's return, was not in a forgiving mood. It was Wednesday, close to the hour when the ball would begin, and although the snow had been melting away all day and the roads open for more than the eight or so hours required for George's return from Yorkshire, there was yet no word from him. *If some dreadful accident hasn't killed him,* Bernard fumed, *then I surely will!*

A tap on the door stopped his brooding. "Come in," he called, wheeling his chair about to face the door, hope springing up in his chest for the hundredth time that day.

Pratkin stepped gingerly into the room and threw his master an uneasy glance.

Bernard understood the look at once. "Damnation!" he swore. "Nothing?"

"Not a word," the valet said. "His man hasn't heard anything since his lordship left for Yorkshire on Thursday."

Bernard's body seemed to sag in the chair. "That's it, then. I may as well go to bed."

Pratkin stepped in front of the wheelchair. "Over my dead body," he declared, crossing his arms over his chest in a stance of stubborn immobility. "You can jolly well go to the ball without him."

"Indeed?" Bernard's brows lifted haughtily. "And when did you become master in this house?"

"You always say I rule the roost," the valet said, jutting out his chin belligerently. "So let's make it true, this once."

"We'll make it *un*true this once! I'm not going, and that's that. So stand aside and let me pass."

The valet didn't budge. "Just give me one good reason why you can't go by yourself. Don't you see, sir, that by not going, you're only cutting off your nose to spite your face?"

"Do you really think, Pratkin," Bernard asked in disgust, "that a silly cliché will make me change my mind?"

"Then perhaps a simple fact with change it—the fact that a very nice young lady, Miss Harriet Renwood by name, visited you here especially to make sure you'd attend. Do you really want to hurt her?"

Bernard's eyes fell. *Would I hurt her?* he asked himself again. *Does she truly want me to come, or is she just being kind?* Caught between his desires and his fears, he was unable to make a decision. "Do you really think my absence would hurt her?" he found himself asking his man.

Pratkin recognized a capitulation when he heard one. "She wouldn't have come here if she didn't care, now would she?" Without waiting for an answer, he marched firmly round to the back of the chair and wheeled Bernard toward the door. "I've your evening clothes all laid out. You can be ready in half an hour."

An hour later, Bernard's carriage drew up in front of the Renwood townhouse. His coachman had to perform some tricky maneuvers to get the carriage close to the door, for the street was clogged with traffic. Pratkin helped his master to alight. When his crutches were properly adjusted, Bernard threw his man a glance that said as clearly as words *I think we've made a terrible mistake;* nevertheless, he started toward the crowded doorway. Pratkin followed. "Don't worry, sir," the valet whispered in his ear. "We'll be waiting right here, if you should need us."

The stairway to the ballroom was a decided squeeze,

but since most people are willing to stand aside for a
person on crutches, he managed to make his way up
without too much difficulty. Just inside the ballroom
doorway, Lord and Lady Renwood and Harriet stood
receiving their guests. Lady Renwood squealed in surprise at Bernard's appearance. "Ah, you've come after
all!" she exclaimed in delight. "That must mean our dear
Frobisher returned in time. But where is he?"

"No, he didn't make it, my lady," Bernard said. "I
decided to brave it on my own."

Harriet gave him a glowing smile. "Good for you, Bernard," she said, taking his hand in hers. "I'm so happy
you did!"

Her words and her smile warmed him. For the first
time that evening, he felt glad he'd come. He wanted to
lift her hand to his lips, but the press of incoming guests
behind him prevented it. He had to relinquish her hand
and get out of the way.

He hobbled over to the sidelines of the dance floor.
The dancing had already begun, and the air rang with
music and laughing voices. The row of gilded chairs along
the walls were sparsely occupied; here and there a group
of elderly ladies gossiped together, and a few old gentlemen whose dancing days were long past stood watching
the lively scene before them. Bernard looked about carefully, hoping to spy an acquaintance with whom he could
chat, but so far he could see not one familiar face. With
nothing better to do, he kept his eyes on the doorway,
where Harriet still remained welcoming the incoming
guests. After a few moments, however, the crowd at the
doorway thinned. Bernard watched in frustration as a
foppish fellow took Harriet out of the receiving line and
led her, smiling, to the dance floor. It was a waltz. Harriet
made a charming sight as she whirled about the floor,
her mauve silk gown billowing about her. But all Bernard
could do was to stand there hanging on his crutches,
gawking at her and looking pathetic. In spite of the pleasant beginning, this evening was turning out to be, just as
he'd feared, a deuced nightmare.

By the time the waltz ended, and a new line was forming for a country dance, the floor had become so crowded that he could no longer see Harriet in the melee. He did think he caught a glimpse of her mauve gown amid a circle of giggling females, but he wasn't sure. Since it would be torture, anyway, to watch her swinging about in some other fellow's arms, he decided to sit down on one of the chairs. He'd just set aside his crutches and made himself comfortable when a pert young lady with a head covered with lively little curls came up to him. "Isn't this your name on my dance card?" she asked, holding the card out to him.

"I don't think so, miss," he said. "I couldn't have—" But a glance at the card, at the third line where she was pointing, revealed the name Bernard Tretheway in large letters. He looked up at the girl in surprise. "That is my name, I admit, but I don't know how it got there." He pointed to the crutches leaning on the wall behind him. "As you may notice, I can't dance."

"Oh, I know that," the girl said cheerfully as she perched on an empty chair beside him. "The little check mark next to your name means that we sit out this dance. My name is Mary Gibbons, by the way."

"How do you do, Miss Gibbons? Forgive me for not rising to bow. But do tell me, how does one 'sit out' a dance?"

She cocked her head at him. "How do you sit out a card game?"

"I'm not familiar with the expression. I suppose it means you don't play the round."

"Exactly!"

"Ah!" He nodded to show he understood, but not fully. "But in this case, what do you do instead?"

"Just this. We sit and chat." She leaned toward him eagerly. "I'm told you are interested in politics, sir. You may not credit it, but so am I. In fact, I am a member of the Ladies Society for Free Schools, and I'm hoping that you gentlemen of the House will stop wrangling over the issue and award funds . . ."

Bernard eyed the young lady with some amusement as she proceeded to try to educate him on the matter of charity school funding, an issue on which he'd recently given a full-hour speech. He did not interrupt her to tell her he was well informed on the subject but let her ramble on. She did not run out of words for the entire time of the dance, but when it was over she ceased her rodomontade immediately. "I must go," she said, jumping up, "but it's been a pleasure to meet you,"

"And to meet you, too," Bernard said with a grin.

As he watched her walk away, he wondered how she'd learned his name. Her reason for "sitting out" the dance with him seemed apparent: she wanted to win him to her side of the charity-school funding debate, not knowing that he was already on her side. He sat back in his chair, the smile engendered by the girl's enthusiasm still lingering on his face.

The smile was doomed to fade, however, for within another few seconds, another female came up to him and showed him her dance card. There was his name, with a check mark beside it. He gawked at her in astonishment. This young lady, a plump, blue-eyed lass with full, dimpled cheeks, blushed with shyness. "I'm Cissy," she said.

"Are you, indeed?" Bernard studied her with knit brows. "And are you supposed to 'sit out' this dance with me?"

"Yes, sir, if it pleases you," the girl said diffidently.

"It pleases me greatly. Won't you sit down?"

The girl took a seat and cast him an uneasy glance. "This is a very nice party, don't you agree?" she asked.

"Yes, very," he responded politely.

"A great squeeze."

"Yes."

There was an awkward pause. Then the girl said, in a tone of nervous desperation, "The music is . . . er . . . lovely, is it not?"

Bernard tried hard not to laugh. "And the weather is very fine, too," he said, straight-faced.

The girl blinked at him. "But it's so cold!" Then, noting the amusement in his eyes, she gave a little hiccoughing laugh. "Oh, you're teasing me."

"Yes," he said, smiling at her.

She sighed and looked down at her hands that were folded in her lap. "I'm not very good at making conversation. I never know what is the proper thing to say."

"Perhaps you shouldn't worry about being proper. What would you like to say that might be improper?"

She looked up at him wonderingly. "Do you really think I should try it? Saying something really improper, I mean?"

"Yes, I do," he assured her. "Really."

She gulped. "Then, I'd like to ask if . . . if . . ."

"Go on," he prodded. "Ask."

"If your legs are . . . if they hurt you."

The question surprised him. "No," he said frankly. "It was a long time ago that I was injured."

She looked at him worriedly. "Was that question very improper?"

"No," he said, after considering the question for a moment. "Actually, I rather like your asking it. Most people pretend that my incapacity doesn't exist."

"Then would you like to tell me how it happened?"

"Do you really want to know?"

She nodded eagerly. "It would make this a real conversation, wouldn't it? Not just shy silliness about the weather."

He agreed and gave her a brief account of the incident of his fall. She kept prodding for more details, keeping the conversation so interesting to them both that they were disappointed when the music stopped, indicating that the dance had ended. The girl rose reluctantly. "Now I have to dance with Freddie Gladstone," she murmured, frowning at her dance card. "I never know what to say to him."

"Just be improper," Bernard reminded her. "You'll be fine."

She laughed, blew him a kiss, and ran off.

He was not surprised when a third young lady appeared before him. He was beginning to understand what machinations were afoot. This lady was tall and slender, a dark-eyed beauty in a peach-colored, shimmery gown that clung shamelessly to her breast and hip bones. "I suppose my name is on your dance card," he said to her. "With a check mark after it."

She nodded, slid gracefully onto the chair beside his, and stretched her legs so far out in front of her that her slim ankles were revealed. "Aaah," she sighed, "how good it feels to sit down."

"Too much dancing?"

"Quite. My last partner kept treading on my toes. What a bore!"

"I may be a bore as well," he said, "but at least I won't tread on your toes."

She turned in her chair and looked at him speculatively. "We could avoid boredom, you know, by just not forcing ourselves to converse. Would you mind if I just closed my eyes and rested for a bit?"

"Not at all," he said. "What better way to spend a sit-out?"

The girl closed her eyes and actually nodded off. Bernard had to shake her shoulder when the music stopped. "Your next partner will be looking for you," he told her when she opened her eyes.

"Sorry," she said languidly, and she languidly rose and languidly wandered off.

What a bore, Bernard said to himself as watched her make her undulating way across the dance floor.

He had barely a moment in which to wonder who would next be "sitting out" with him when she appeared before him. She was the prettiest of the lot so far, with coppery curls that fell about her face and a pair of eyes of the lightest blue. "I'm Elaine Whitmore," she said with a flirtatious smile. "Your name is on my dance card."

"Yes, I know," he said. "With a check mark after it. Meaning this is a 'sit-out.' I can't dance, you know."

"Oh, I know all about you," she said, dropping down

on the chair beside him. "I've just returned from a week-end in Yorkshire, where your friend, Lord Chadleigh, was one of the guests."

"Good God! *George?*" He gaped at her. "You were at Felicia's with George?"

"Yes. Yes, I was."

"Then where the devil is he? If you made it here to-night, why didn't he?"

"I'm sure I couldn't say," Elaine said. "He disappeared on Sunday without saying good-bye to anyone. I believe he went to Scotland."

"Scotland?" The anger that he'd felt all day returned in full force. "What possessed him to do that?"

"I'm not sure. I think it had something to do with Felicia's friend who lives there. But, Sir Bernard, I'd like to ask you a few questions about your friend George. Do you think he might be a bit thoughtless in his dealings with the female sex?"

"Thoughtless?" Bernard felt his teeth clench. "I think he's thoughtless in *all* his dealings, damn him!" He drew in a deep breath to regain control of his temper. "I beg your pardon, Miss . . . er . . . Whitmore, is it? . . . for my rude language, but I think it best that we avoid discussing George at this moment. Instead, why don't you explain to me how my name appeared on your dance card."

Elaine eyed him curiously. "Harriet Renwood put it there, of course. She signed your name on the cards of several of her friends. Didn't you know?"

"Yes, I suppose I did. Did she also give you instructions as to how to deal with me?"

"Not exactly. She only said to be sure we sat with you for the length of a dance and that we made pleasant company for you."

With his teeth clenched even tighter, Bernard reached for his crutches. "Thank you, Miss Whitmore, for giving me your time. When you next see Miss Renwood, assure her that you, and the other young ladies who 'sat out' with me, were pleasant indeed."

Elaine could not miss the fury in his voice. "But, sir," she asked in alarm, "you're not leaving, are you?"

"At once," he said shortly, heaving himself up on his crutches.

"But there are at least four more ladies who have your name on their cards!"

"That is to be regretted, I'm sure," he snapped as he hobbled off, "but they'll have to find another fellow to 'sit out' with them."

As he made his way around the dance floor to the doorway, Bernard grew more and more enraged. It was becoming quite clear to him what Harriet's intentions had been. Not wishing to indulge him this time as she'd done that wonderful evening when she'd not left his side, she'd passed him on to her friends. She'd divided up the chore (for surely making conversation with a cripple had to be considered a chore) into neat little parcels of time—the length of one dance. He could almost hear her giving instructions to her friends: *"Surely you can spare one dance to make the poor fellow happy."* Maybe she'd even hoped that one of her friends might take to him. Then Harriet herself wouldn't have to feel so sorry for him.

He was halfway down the stairs to the outer door when he heard his name called from above. "Bernard! You can't be leaving!"

He did not need to look back. He recognized Harriet's voice. "Yes, I can," he said angrily as he continued his laborious descent. "Thank you for an entertaining evening."

"But the evening is far from over."

"It is for me." He continued his awkward way down the stairs, uncomfortably aware that the two footmen, standing stony-faced at each side of the doorway, could hear every word.

Harriet was too distressed to concern herself about the footmen. She lifted her skirts and ran down the stairs after him. "Please, Bernard, don't go! I need you. Your name is on my dance card. You're to take me in to supper in a little while."

"Sorry. I'm sure you can find someone else to accomp—" In his agitated haste to escape a confrontation with her, he'd misjudged the placement of his left crutch. He'd placed the tip too close to the edge of the stair, and at this moment he leaned his weight on it. The tip slipped, the crutch dropped to the step below, and Bernard, losing his balance, tumbled down the three remaining steps and landed flat on his face on the entryway floor.

Harriet screamed in horror. The two footmen ran across to him, but Harriet, having flown down the stairs, motioned them aside and knelt down beside him. "Bernard, speak to me!' she cried. "Are you hurt?"

"*Hurt?*" Poor Bernard almost laughed at the word. His chin was throbbing, his elbow was giving off sharp pains, and he was sprawled like a speared fish on the floor in front of the woman he loved. "No, I'm not hurt," he muttered in an agony of humiliation. "Just permit your footmen to help me up."

He did not look at her while they lifted him up nor when he was restored to self-sufficiency on his crutches. He merely brushed off the helping hands, mumbled thanks to the men, and hobbled out the door.

Harriet watched him go. "Oh, Bernard!" she whispered miserably. That choked whisper expressed all the empathetic pain she was feeling. But only the footmen heard her. They had to turn away, not only from the tormented sound but from the look on her face. Her tear-laden, stricken eyes revealed all the anguish in her heart. If Bernard had turned around and seen her face, he might have found some comfort.

But he wouldn't look back.

Twenty-Three

The night after George had taken his final departure, Livy lay awake mulling over the disastrous few days they had spent together bringing her home. Everything had gone wrong. She hadn't wanted him to take her home in the first place, but she certainly hadn't wished for him to be compelled to stay. She was ashamed of how her uncle ran his household. She'd never invited Felicia or any of her school friends to visit her, nor had she ever told them how dismal her life was. She didn't want her friends to pity her. Even her friends' pity, however, would be more bearable than pity from George. To have him pity her was an unimaginable pain.

Yet circumstances had conspired to bring her worst nightmare about. George had learned firsthand the awful details—that no fires were permitted in most of the rooms, that every servant had to do the work of three, that her uncle was thoughtless and selfish, and, worst of all, that she didn't have the will or the character to assert herself. George had even found it necessary to give her uncle the scolding that she herself should have given him years ago.

Ever since she'd met George, his behavior toward her had troubled her. She didn't know what to make of him. She knew he thought of her as a pathetic spinster, but he nevertheless paid a great deal of attention to her. It was plain that he enjoyed her company. But she knew she had to keep him at arm's length. She was too attracted to him for her own comfort. Nothing but pain could come of an attraction that was doomed to be one-sided. The pain she'd suffered when he kissed her was a warning. She didn't understand why he'd done it, but it had thrilled her to the core. She remembered how, in spite of her intention to free herself from his embrace, she'd melted against him. It had been a delicious moment, and in truth, she would have wanted it to go on forever, but her instincts for self-preservation had come to the fore, and she'd pulled herself away. The only logical reason for him to have kissed her was pity. Kindness—that was the only thing he could offer her, and it was the one thing she couldn't abide his offering.

Ah, but it had been lovely for a moment. A moment she'd have loved to relive. She pulled her comforter close about her and tried to imagine she was in his arms again. And with that, she fell asleep.

The next thing she knew, Bridie was shaking her. She opened her eyes. From the light seeping in between the draperies, she could tell the morning was quite advanced. "What is it?" she asked the abigail sleepily.

"Heesht ye, miss," Bridie said urgently. "Mrs. Nicol be in a curfuffle. Somethin's mishanter wi' yer uncle."

A mishap? Alarmed, Livy threw a robe over her nightdress and ran down to her uncle's room. She found him sitting up at the foot of his bed, staring with dazed eyes straight ahead of him. Mrs. Nicol stood on his right with his bowl of gruel in her hand, and Peters, on the other side, was attempting to put a woolen lap robe over his shoulders. "What is it?" Livy asked. "What's wrong?"

"I found 'im like that at daybreak," Peters muttered. "Don' know how long he's been sittin' here in this icy cold."

"It's as if he doesn't hear a word we say to him," Mrs. Nicol added, "and not only that, but he won't eat a morsel."

Livy sat down beside the grizzled old man and put an arm about his shoulder. "What is it, Uncle? Does something trouble you? A pain, perhaps?"

He turned slowly toward her, as if he were about to speak. Then his eye fell on her bandaged forehead. "Wheesht!" he rasped, peering at her aghast. " 'Twas I did that to ye, didn't I?"

"It was an accident, Uncle. Nothing serious. I'll be removing the bandage this morning."

He took her hand in his. She could feel him shaking. "I wish t' talk to ye, Livy, lass," he said. "Tell the others t' gie owre."

"If you'd not lapse into your Lowlands brogue, you could tell them yourself," Livy suggested, hoping to urge him back to his normal behavior.

The old man frowned at her for a moment and then shrugged. He looked up at his worried housekeeper, at his valet who was still holding on to the shawl, and finally at little Bridie who was watching from the doorway, her tiny mouth pursed with alarm. "I'm fine," he said, a slight note of apology in his tone, "so go away. All of ye."

Mrs. Nicol went promptly to the door, but Peters, with a quick, nervous movement, dropped the lap robe on Sir Andrew's shoulders before scurrying out. Mrs. Nicol paused at the door. "I'll be right outside if you need me, Miss Livy," she declared with flinty resolve.

When the door closed behind them, Livy looked back at her uncle to find that he'd relapsed into the dazed state in which she'd found him. "They're gone," she said, pressing his shoulder firmly to regain his attention. "What is it you want to tell me?"

He seemed to shake himself awake. He leaned toward her and peered closely into her face. "You dinna believe, do ye, Livy, that I was forced to take ye in?"

"Take me in?" she asked, surprised. "Do you mean back when I was a child?"

"Aye."

"I don't know, Uncle. Were you?"

He stiffened in offense. "Nae, I was not. 'Twas my joy to take ye in. My joy, I tell ye! Y' were my dear sister's bairn, and I loved ye from yer birth." Tears filled his eyes. "Do ye recall how I played wi' ye when ye were small? And the birthday parties we had, wi' clotted cream fer the scones? And did I not hire the best tutors for ye, no matter the cost? And when ye turned sixteen, did I not send ye t' the very best girls' school in all England?"

"Yes, you did, Uncle," she said, kissing his forehead. "You were very good to me."

"Then why did that blasted gomerel break into my bedroom yesterday and accuse me of mistreating you? Did you complain to him about me?"

"No, Uncle, you know perfectly well that I'd never do that."

He dropped his eyes from hers. "Aye, I know. He must've seen me bruise yer forehead."

"No. But he bandaged me. I explained to him that it was an accident."

Sir Andrew's brows came together thoughtfully. "Howsomever, he must've seen enough t' conclude that I've been a brute t' ye. And I suppose I have." He eyed her guiltily, a look of sincere regret. "It was when I came on ill, y' see. The chest pains. I thought I was done for. I suppose I turned grumly."

"I wouldn't say grumly, Uncle," Livy said with a smile, patting his hand comfortingly. "More persnickety than ill-natured."

"Whatever ye wish t' call it, the truth is I began t' think more o' myself than o' anyone else. 'Twas from fear, ye see. I didna wish t' die."

"But the doctor says you seem to be in quite good health."

"Aye, so he says." He put a shaking hand to his forehead. "Then how am I to explain meself? Can it be I *like* bein' an invalid?"

"I don't think so, my dear," Livy said hesitantly, aware that something crucial was occurring in the old man's mind. "Perhaps it's only fear, as you say. And you, Uncle, are not the sort to cringe from fear."

The old man took a deep breath. "Nae, I'm not." He

rose slowly to his feet. "Thankee, lass. Things will be different here from now on. I'll not stay abed anither day." In a grand gesture of defiance, he threw the lap robe off his shoulders. "Don't sit there gawkin' at me, lass. Go tell Peters to find my old walkin' stick. And ask him t' bring in my old kilt. I mean t' get myself dressed!"

Livy, exhilarated by this promising conversation, ran to do his bidding. But just as she was about to go out the door, he called her name.

"Yes?" she asked, looking back over her shoulder tensely. Had he changed his mind?

"That fellow who gave me that tongue-lashing yesterday—"

Livy's eyebrows rose. "The 'blasted gomerel'?"

"Aye. What was his name?"

"Frobisher," she said. "George Frobisher, Lord Chadleigh. Why do you ask?"

"Because ye should invite him back."

"Good God, Uncle, whatever for? So that you can return the tongue-lashing he gave you?"

"Nae, lass. Because he's brave and braw. And, if my old eyes dinna deceive me, he dauts on ye."

"He may be brave and handsome, Uncle," she retorted as she scooted from the room, "but if you think he dotes on me, you'd better have the doctor examine those old eyes."

Twenty-Four

At midmorning the next day, the carriage-turned-sleigh finally arrived in London. George was up on the box, weary, unshaven, and chilled to the bone. Timmy was curled up inside on the backseat, taking his turn to sleep. George yearned to fall into his own bed, but his conscience would not permit it. He had to stop first at Bernard's rooms and apologize for breaking his word.

He drew some amused jeers from the passersby as he pulled up in front of Bernard's place, for the sleigh runners—making loud, scraping sounds against the cobbles of the streets that were now almost free of snow—had become embarrassingly unnecessary. Ignoring the jibes, he ran up to the door and knocked urgently. Pratkin responded to his knock. "Ah, your lordship," he said with formal politeness, "welcome back to London."

"Thank you, Pratkin. Is Bernard in his study? I'll run right up."

But Pratkin barred the way. "Sorry, my lord, but Sir Bernard is not receiving today."

George hooted. "Since when does that apply to me? Stand aside, fellow, and let me pass."

"I regret, my lord, that I cannot. Sir Bernard is . . . er . . . sleeping."

"Sleeping?" George asked in disbelief. "At eleven in the morning?"

"Yes, my lord. He retired quite late last night."

"Did he?" George frowned at the valet suspiciously, but slowly his weary eyes brightened. A delightful possibility was dawning on him. "Good God!" he burst out excitedly. "You don't mean—! Are you saying he went to the Renwoods' ball after all?"

Pratkin remained impassive. "Yes, my lord, he did."

"Why, that's *wonderful!*" George pounded the valet on his back with hearty enthusiasm. "The best news I've had all week! Very well, I'll let him sleep. Tell him I'll be back in a few hours to hear all about it."

Without disturbing Timmy, he drove the phaeton home, the runners scraping the almost-dry streets roughly. As he came scrunching into his driveway, he saw Harriet Renwood emerging from his front door. He jumped down from the box and ran over to her. "Harriet," he greeted her cheerfully, "were you paying me a call?"

"Oh, George, you're back!" she said with a strange little quiver in her voice. "Your butler just informed me that you were still in Yorkshire."

"I only this moment returned," he said.

"We had hoped," Harriet murmured, dropping her eyes from his face, "that you'd be back yesterday."

"I'd hoped so, too, but we were forced to take a long detour. However, my delay was not as damaging to our plans as I feared." He smiled down at her. "I'm told that Bernard attended your ball without me."

"Yes." She looked up at him but did not return his smile. "That's why I'm here. I must speak to you."

George, noting the troubled look in her eyes, immediately tensed. Something unfortunate must have happened at the ball. "Of course," he said, "if you don't mind coming back inside and sitting down with me in all my dirt."

She merely nodded and let him lead her inside. The butler came running to the door, ready to offer his returning master a warm welcome, but George held up a restraining hand. "Yes, Wesley, I'm back," he said quickly, "but I'll not be needing you for a while. Miss

Renwood and I will be in the library. Will you please give Timmy a hand with the carriage and then get him to bed? By that time, I think, Miss Renwood and I will be ready for some tea."

George and Harriet didn't speak as they walked down the hall to the library. It was not until he'd taken her cloak and settled her on an armchair in front of the fire that he asked the urgent question: "Tell me at once, Harriet, what happened last night?"

"It was a disaster," she said in a choked voice. "Bernard had such a dreadful time that he left after a mere hour's stay. And when I ran to the stairway to urge him to come back, he . . . he"—at this point she couldn't hold back her tears—"he *fell*!"

"Good God!" George's breath caught in his chest. "Was he hurt?"

"I don't think so. He managed to get to his carriage without any help. And when I went to his rooms this morning, his man assured me he was well."

George felt a surge of relief, but this information evidently was not as soothing to Harriet as it should have been, for he saw her shoulders slump and her eyes tear up again. "Are you trying to say that you don't believe he's truly well?" he asked her.

"If he were, why wouldn't his m-man let m-me see him?"

"I don't know. As a matter of fact, now you mention it, Pratkin didn't let me in either."

There was something alarming about all this. George got up and paced about the room, trying to get his tired brain to *think*. Harriet, nervous and upset, pulled off a glove and used it to dab at her wet cheeks while she waited for a response. At last George, deciding that he had to comfort her despite his own misgivings, drew up a chair close to hers and sat down. "I don't think you need worry," he said, taking her gloved hand in his. "If Bernard managed to get down the stairs and out to his carriage on his own, there can't have been any bones broken."

"I suppose not," she said, still not comforted, "but, you see, George, Bernard's fall isn't my only concern."

"No?"

She took a deep breath. "I don't understand him, George, not at all." And, suddenly, a flood of words came pouring out of her. "He told me, a few days ago, that he would not attend the dance without your company. When it became clear that you'd been delayed, I offered my brother as a companion. Bernard refused, so I assumed he would not come. When he did appear— and on his own!—I was truly delighted. I thought it meant . . ." She hesitated, a bit of color rising in her cheeks.

"You thought—?" he prodded.

"Oh, never mind what I thought. But as one of the hostesses, I was beset with social obligations and could not keep him company all evening. So I devised a plan to keep him amused until I could be free. But he evidently took offense, though I cannot imagine why."

"What sort of plan did you devise?"

"I'd arranged for six of my friends to sit out a dance with him," she explained, resorting again to playing with her glove. "Then, for the last dance before supper, I planned to keep him company myself and then go to supper with him." She rubbed her forehead in pained bewilderment. "I tell you, George, I'm completely at sea. What was wrong with my plan? How could it have offended him?"

"I have no idea," George admitted. "It seems a very good plan to me."

"That's what I thought. But after only four dances, he left in a fury."

George tried to imagine himself in his friend's situation as Harriet had described it. "Could one of your friends have offended him?" he wondered.

"I suppose it's possible," Harriet said, "though I questioned all four. Every one of them declared that the time was spent very pleasantly. In fact, Cissy Glendale, who's very tongue-tied in the company of gentlemen, said that

Bernard made it delightfully easy for her to converse . . . that the time she spent with him was the best part of her evening. Of course, it was later—when he was with Elaine Whitmore—that he stormed off."

"Elaine Whitmore?" This took George by surprise. "Was *she* there?"

"Yes. Why? Do you know her?"

"I've met the lady," he said dryly. "She has a very— how shall I say?—*determined* way about her. She might very well make a fellow storm off."

"Do you think so?" Harriet brightened in relief at the possibility that someone else might be at fault, but the relief lasted only for a moment. Then she shook her head. "I don't know, George. I had the impression he was furious with *me,* not with any of my friends."

George shrugged helplessly. "I can't think of any other reason—"

"Please, George," she begged, pressing his hand urgently, "will you speak to him for me? That's what I've come to ask you. Go to him, and explain that I wished only to make his evening pleasant."

He readily agreed. "I'll go to him right away," he promised.

Having achieved her purpose, Harriet rose and put on her cloak. He walked with her down the hall to the outer doorway, paying no heed to the astonished butler who was on his way to the library with the tea tray. At the door, George urged her not to worry. "Everything is bound to turn out well," he said with a cheerfulness he did not feel. "You'll see."

Twenty-Five

As soon as Harriet was gone, George, without taking the time to wash or shave or change his clothes, strode past the startled Wesley (still holding his tea tray) and left the house. Despite his utter weariness, he hurried through the few streets between his house and Bernard's rooms and burst in the door. This time, when Pratkin tried to stop him, he brushed past the fellow and stamped up the stairs to Bernard's study.

Bernard had been sitting in his wheelchair, staring unseeingly out the window at the little square garden behind his building. When he heard the door burst open, he wheeled himself about. "Dash it, I told you not to disturb—" he began. At the sight of George, standing in the doorway glaring at him, he gaped, startled.

But George was startled, too. Bernard's chin and left cheek were disfigured with a large bluish bruise. "Good God," he cried, "you *are* hurt!"

"It's nothing," Bernard said. "Just a black-and-blue mark. It will heal."

George slowly approached him and gave the bruised face a close examination. "Is this the full extent of it?" he demanded to know. "Any other injuries?"

Bernard would not answer. He spun his chair around, rudely turning his back to his visitor. "I'm not speaking to you," he said.

George spun the chair back. "But I'm speaking to you," he said, taking firm hold of the arms of the chair so that Bernard couldn't turn away again. "I know I broke my promise, and I'm sorry. But it couldn't be helped."

"Couldn't it? Isn't it true that instead of keeping your word, you chose to escort some lady to Scotland? Was it the lovely lady of mystery you went to Yorkshire to meet? Was it she who kept you from honoring your pledge and coming home?"

"Yes, yes, and yes. All true."

"Am I supposed to forgive you for that self-indulgence?"

"It was not self-indulgence," George snapped. "It was a necessity."

"Are you saying that coming home to keep your promise to me was *not* a necessity?"

"Damnation, Bernard, that necessity was only a *ball*! The trip to Scotland was a . . . a life crisis!"

"Well, the blasted ball turned into a life crisis for me," Bernard muttered bitterly. "I fell on my face right in front of her."

"So I hear. Which reminds me that you didn't answer my question about the accident. Were there any other injuries?"

"Only a bruise to my elbow. And my pride." Bernard's brow suddenly furrowed. "You *knew* about all this when you stormed in here. *How?* Did Pratkin gabble the whole to you?"

"No, it was Harriet herself. She came to see me. She's quite upset, you know."

Bernard wrenched the wheelchair from George's grasp and wheeled himself over to the window. "She'll get over it," he muttered.

George followed him. "I don't see why you're so put out with her. She tried to make the ball pleasant for you. When she came to see me, she was in tears over your fall. It seems to me that she shows every sign of caring for you."

"No, she doesn't care. Not in the way I'd hoped she would." He gave a deep sigh. "It's over, George."

"How can you be sure of that?"

"I'm sure. If she cared for me, would she have paraded out all her available friends for my inspection? It's plain she wanted to pass me over to one of them."

George couldn't answer. He felt instinctively that Bernard was mistaken, but mere instinct would not make a good argument. With a hopeless shrug, he pulled a chair over to the window and sat down beside his friend. "It's a damnable shame," he mumbled.

Bernard glanced at him and noticed for the first time his friend's disheveled appearance. "Good God, man," he exclaimed, "you look awful."

George laughed. "You're a fine one to talk."

Bernard smiled back at him ruefully. "There's a reason for my disfigurement. But you! What excuse have you? Did you forget how to shave?"

George rubbed his scraggly chin. "I drove my blasted phaeton for two days without stopping. Then, immediately on my return, I became entangled in your affairs. When was I to shave?"

"Two days? Without stopping?" Bernard asked, impressed. "All the way from Scotland?"

"Well, I did *try* to make it back on time," George answered softly.

Bernard, chastened, put out his hand. "Very well. You're forgiven."

They shook hands. Relieved that the animosity was over, they held the clasp tightly for a long moment. Then George got up. "This calls for a drink," he said. "I'll call Pratkin."

He threw open the door and discovered Pratkin right outside. Before George could accuse him of eavesdropping, the valet quickly said, "I'll bring the drinks at once. Shall it be port?"

"Bring the good Scotch, you snooper," Bernard ordered. "A whole bottle."

In a very short time they were both feeling mellow. "I'm truly sorry 'bout Harriet," George remarked, staring glumly at the empty glass in his hand.

" 'S not your fault," Bernard assured him. "Wouldn't've been any diff'rent if you'd been there."

"Might've been."

"She doesn't care f' me. I'd've learned it sooner 'r later."

"Hmmm," was all George said. But he wasn't at all sure his friend was right.

"What about y'r lovely lady in Scotland?" Bernard asked.

"What about her?"

"Does she care f' you?"

George drained his glass. "She hates me."

"No!"

"Yes!" He picked up the bottle and poured himself another drink. "Took me in dislike from th' first."

Bernard shook his head. "We're a sad pair, I mus' say."

"But at least we're still a pair."

"Right!" Bernard said. "The devil take the fair sex." He lifted his glass. "To us."

"To us," George echoed, and downed his drink. "Who needs women?"

Twenty-Six

*T*he next day, no longer showing any signs of inebria-
tion (but suffering a punishing headache to remind
him of his dissipation), George went to call on Harriet
as he'd promised. It was an awkward interview. Although
he assured her that Bernard was not seriously hurt, and
that he did not in any way blame Harriet for his fall,
George nevertheless had to advise her that it would not
be wise for her to see him for a time. When Harriet
demanded to know why, he could only answer that Bernard was feeling "peckish," and wanted to avoid company. Harriet, disappointed and heart-sore, could do
nothing but accept the advice.

Having pledged to avoid women, the two friends spent
the ensuing weeks in lonely isolation. The month of December, until the Christmas season, was quiet in London,
so invitations were few, and if they included females,
neither George nor Bernard would accept them. And
since Parliament was not due to resume until January,
even their clubs were thin of interesting company. The
only companionship they had was each other, and though
neither would admit it, by the end of the year they were
each becoming bored with the other.

For George, the only interesting event of the month
was a letter from his sister that arrived just before Christmas. He was in the morning room having his breakfast
when Wesley brought it to him. Felicia had written:

Dearest Georgie,

*As you know I'm not fond of letter-writing, but
Leyton insists that you will find my writing
style more enjoyable than his. I don't know why
he says so. He writes very good letters. One of
them was even printed in the Times, which is certainly more than I can claim. But, obedient to
his wishes, I'm writing this myself to inform you
that Leyton and I will be returning to London
right after the New Year. You know, Georgie,
how much I love living in the country, but it
does become distressingly dull in the winter when
one doesn't get many visitors. Most of my
friends are already in town, so I shall be quite
busy soon after my arrival, even though the
season will not have fully begun. We plan to arrive at Leyton House on the third, so I expect
you to call on us immediately thereon. I have a
great deal of news to disclose to you, and Leyton is eager to speak to you on parliamentary
matters, so you are not to keep us waiting.*

*Don't be surprised if, when you come, you find
us already entertaining a guest. My friend Livy
(Miss Olivia Henshaw whom you were so kind
as to escort to Scotland last month, remember?) is coming down for a month's holiday in
town and has agreed to stay with us.*

*Speaking of my friends, I wonder if you know
that Elaine Whitmore is in town, staying with
her mother on Dover Street? I hope it isn't a
breach of honor if I hint to you she would be
delighted to have you call on her.*

Your loving sister, Felicia.

It was not that Felicia's babble (a message that could
have been put in six words—*we're coming to London
January third*—was sprawled over two pages) was in itself
particularly interesting. But one bit of the letter caught

him by surprise and actually made his pulse quicken. Livy was coming to London!

He read the sentence over and over. *Miss Olivia Henshaw whom you were so kind as to escort to Scotland last month, remember?* (Remember? As if he could ever forget!) *is coming to town.* Those few words provoked a turmoil in his mind. Wild speculations, intriguing possibilities, and puzzling questions swirled through his brain like bees in a hive. Livy was coming! How was it possible? Why had her uncle permitted it? Had his own insulting, uncalled-for diatribe actually had an effect on the monstrous Sir Andrew? That seemed unlikely. What was more likely was the possibility that the old fellow had passed away. But if that was true, would Livy give herself a holiday so soon after the event? That did not seem likely either.

Whatever the answers, Felicia's letter made one thing clear: Livy was coming! He would be seeing her again . . . and in less than a week. He felt like getting up and dancing round the table. The paper in his hand was actually shaking.

The paper was shaking. He suddenly took notice of the trembling of his hand. He blinked at it in astonishment. Why, he wondered, was his hand trembling? What did it mean? What was causing this overwrought feeling of both agitation and excited anticipation?

He got up and paced about the room until a possible explanation occurred to him. The possibility made his knees strangely weak. *Good God,* he thought in shock, sinking back down on his chair, *can I be in love with someone I once believed was a dried-up old spinster?*

Twenty-Seven

*O*n the third of January, as promised, Felicia and Leyton came down to London and settled into their townhouse on Grosvenor Street. A few days later Livy arrived. She was driven up to the Leyton House door in a shiny new coach. Kelby, who'd come out to assist her to descend, was surprised by the new carriage, for he remembered vividly the shabby old barouche in which she'd arrived at the Abbey not many weeks before. And when he saw her climb down wearing an elegant cloak with a fur-trimmed hood, followed by Bridie carrying a shiny new bandbox, he wondered if Miss Henshaw had suddenly come into money.

After sending Bridie off with two footmen to assist her, Kelby led the new arrival to the sitting room, where Felicia had been engrossed in examining the new fashions illustrated in *La Belle Assemblée*. At the sight of her guest, Felicia jumped up, tossed aside the magazine, ran across the room, and embraced her with enthusiasm. "Livy, dearest! I'm so delighted that you've come!" she cried excitedly. "I've been longing for your company."

Kelby cleared his throat. "Shall I serve tea, m'lady?"

"Yes, of course, but not right at this moment." She turned to her friend. "Livy, love, before we sit down for tea and a good coze, do come upstairs and let me show you the room I've prepared for you."

Livy followed her to the stairs. As they climbed up, Felicia revealed some exciting news. "You won't believe it, but something delightful has resulted from my house party last month. Beatrice Rossiter is going to marry Algy Thomsett!"

"Oh, my!" Livy exclaimed. "That *is* delightful news. I think it a lovely match—he so shy and she so . . . so . . ."

"So nattering," Felicia supplied, laughing. "Yes, I do believe it is a good pairing. And it proves I have some talent as a matchmaker, no matter what Leyton says." They reached the second floor and proceeded down the hall. "I'm giving a dinner party to celebrate the betrothal, and—"

But they'd arrived at the guest room. Felicia threw open the door. "There!" she announced proudly. "I've had it done especially for you. I hope you like it."

Livy looked round, wide-eyed. The room was large and bright, with windows facing Grosvenor Square. The furnishings were charming, the lace draperies at the windows and over the bed frame were fit for a queen, and Felicia had placed an enormous bowl of yellow winter mums on the bedside table as a special welcome. Livy, whose bedroom at home was a dark, unadorned chamber like a cell in a nunnery, was overwhelmed. "Oh, how lovely," she sighed happily.

"I want you to make yourself completely at home," Felicia urged. "I've put Bridie in a room right next to you, and of course my abigail will always be available to you. Don't be shy about asking for anything you desire."

"I can't imagine that I'll be wanting for a thing," Livy assured her, gesturing at the dressing table laden with soaps and lotions and perfumes. She took a seat at it and began to untie her bonnet.

Felicia came up behind her friend and examined her in the mirror. "You look so very well!" she exclaimed as soon as Livy had removed the hat. "You're not wearing that dreadful spinster's cap. Without it, you look ten years younger than when I saw you last."

"I doubt that"—Livy laughed—"but I do admit that I'm not as strained as I was. Life has been a bit easier for me of late."

"Has it really? Your uncle is better, then?"

"Yes. Much better."

Felicia perched on the bed. "I guessed as much when you wrote that he was permitting you to come to town—and for a whole month!"

Livy turned round on the chair. "I can hardly believe the change in him," she said, her voice revealing her inner amazement. "He doesn't remain in bed all day, as he was used to. He gets up every morning and lets Peters dress him in proper clothes instead of merely a robe. And he actually takes a stroll in the garden when the weather permits, though there haven't been many days during this past December that would entice anyone out of doors." She shook her head as if she still couldn't believe her own words. "He's so changed it seems almost a miracle. And do you know who brought it about? Your brother!"

"*What?*" Felicia gaped at her. "My *Georgie?*"

"Yes, your Georgie. Did he not tell you what he did?"

"No. Not a word. When he came to call the other day, I asked him about his trip to Scotland. All he would say was that it snowed and delayed his return."

"There was a great deal more to the delay than that," Livy said.

"Tell me!" Eagerly, Felicia tucked up her knees and settled in to hear the tale. "Tell me *all!*"

Livy was perfectly willing to do so. "George was snowed in, you know, and very unhappy at being delayed. As soon as the snowstorm passed, he and his tiger set off for London. I was sure I'd seen the last of him. But a few hours later—I can't imagine why—he came back. I heard him running up the stairs. I didn't know it was he, of course, but as soon as I reached the corridor outside my uncle's bedroom, I learned from the butler what had happened. George had driven back to the castle, dashed up to my uncle's bedroom, thrown Peters—my uncle's valet—out of the room, and bolted the door. When I got there, Peters and McTavish were trying to get in, but the door is huge and heavy. Though we could hear George shouting, we couldn't make out what he was saying. He evidently gave my uncle a devastating tongue-lashing. Then he came out, rushed past us, and was off again. Did you ever hear the like?"

"My Georgie did that?" Felicia asked in disbelief. "I can't credit it! I've never known him to be a rudesby."

"Perhaps it was rude," Livy granted, "but my uncle has not been the same man since that day. He's still gruff, of course, but what is most wonderful is how loving he's been to me. Behind the gruff exterior, he's suddenly begun to show concern for me. He puts shawls over my shoulders. He asks me if I've slept well or if I'd dined. He actually insisted that I make this trip. He says I must have some enjoyment of life before it is too late."

"Amazing!" Felicia's brow knit thoughtfully. "And you think it was Georgie's words that made the change?"

"What else could it have been?" Livy turned back to the dressing table and stared at herself in the mirror. "One of my most important purposes in coming to town," she said quietly, "is to thank George for what he did." She lowered her head, leaning her forehead on the glass. "I was not very polite to him during his stay, I'm afraid."

"Oh, pooh. Georgie is not the sort who would want thanks."

"Perhaps not. But I must do it anyway, for my own peace of mind." She turned and gave her hostess a small but determined smile. "If you'll give me his direction, I'll do it tomorrow."

On the morrow, however, George received another visitor. On his return from a brisk canter in the park, he discovered Harriet Renwood, whom he'd not seen all month, standing in his doorway, hesitating to knock. He saw that she was in tears again. "Good heavens, Harriet, what's amiss?" he asked. She was too choked to answer, so he led her inside, ushering her down the hall to the library and into a chair. It took several minutes before she regained control of her emotions. "It's your deuced friend Bernard," she said when she was at last able to speak calmly.

"I surmised as much. What did he do this time?"

"It's what he didn't do." She took a deep breath. "I was walking down Regent Street, on an errand for Mama, when I saw him on the opposite side. I called to him, but he kept walking. So I ran after him. I actually crossed the road and ran after him!" She paused and took another breath.

"And?" George prodded.

"I planted myself right before him," she said tightly, trying not to cry again, "and I said, 'Good morning, Bernard.' And he . . . he . . ."

"Yes?"

She could not stop another burst into tears. "He t-told m-me to *s-s-step aside and l-let him p-p-pass!*" And she dropped her head in her hands and succumbed to heart-rending sobs.

"Please don't cry, Harriet," George begged. He felt completely inadequate to deal with this outpouring. The only thing he could think of to do was to offer sympathy. He knelt down before her and took her hands. "Bernard doesn't . . . he didn't . . . Don't cry, Harriet, please!"

At that moment, the library door opened. Wesley, leading Livy into the room, was saying, "You may wait here, Miss Henshaw. His lordship is sure to be back in a—" At the sight of his master on his knees before a weeping woman, he stopped short.

George leaped up and wheeled about, his heart pounding. "Livy!" he cried in delighted surprise.

But Livy, equally surprised, could not show an equal delight. She paled, and a hand flew up to cover her gaping mouth. There was a moment of stunned silence. Then she mumbled awkwardly, "I'm dreadfully sorry . . . this intrusion . . . I didn't know . . . I'll be back some other time," and she fled.

"I wasn't told you had company, my lord," the butler mumbled, hastily backing out and closing the door.

George took a step toward the door, wanting to cry

out, "Livy, wait!" But the door was firmly closed, the sound of running footsteps already far away, and Harriet was sitting behind him, waiting for his attention. Reluctantly, his mind in a whirl, he turned back to her.

She was leaning forward, looking up at him. Her cheeks still wet with tears, but her eyes were puzzled. "Did my presence cause you some difficulty?" she asked worriedly.

"No, of course not," he said, trying to regain his equilibrium.

"Is that woman a friend of yours?"

He blinked at her. "Woman?"

"You called her Livy."

He felt his fingers clench. "The 'woman' is a friend of my sister's," he said shortly.

Harriet peered at him. "Heavens, have I offended you, too?"

"What makes you ask that?"

"I don't know. Something about your manner. It's changed since that little interruption."

She was right. He had to pull himself together. "Then let's change it back," he said, trying to concentrate on her problem. "We were speaking of Bernard."

"Yes. I was describing to you how he gave me the cut direct." She wiped her cheeks and sat back in her chair. "When you and I last spoke of him, George, you explained that he needed some time to get over being 'peckish.' A month has passed since then, and from this morning's evidence, he seems in a state a great deal worse than peckish. He's terribly angry at me and shows no sign of getting over it. Please, George, you must tell me what it is I've done wrong."

George didn't know how to answer. "I don't understand it myself, Harriet. You must ask him."

"How can I ask him if he won't speak to me?"

George felt helpless, trapped in a situation that was beyond him. He wanted only for this interview to end. Suddenly weary to the bone, he sank down on the sofa opposite her chair. "I don't know," he said glumly.

"Yes, you do. It had something to do with the sit-outs with my friends. What was it, George? He must have told you, his best friend."

"But surely you don't wish me to betray a confidence," he pleaded weakly.

"Yes, I do, if that is what it will take to end this nightmare."

George sighed in defeat. "He has the idea that you paraded your friends before him in order to pass him on to one of them," he said. And to himself he added, *Forgive me, Bernard, but I'm too distracted to know quite what I'm doing.*

"Pass him on?" Harriet peered at him with a sudden intensity. "Did he mean that I wanted him to *pursue* one of them?"

"Yes, I suppose so," George muttered.

"What a ridiculous notion! If I wanted him to pursue some other girl, why would I have—?" She stopped herself and, her eyes fixed blankly on George's face, slowly rose from the chair.

"What is it?" George asked, his attention caught. "Has some solution occurred to you?"

"Perhaps," she said absently, making her way to the door. "I have to go home and think about it."

He rose to see her out. "Won't you tell me what you're thinking? That's the least you can do to console me for betraying his confidence."

She shook her head. "No, I won't tell you. But George—" Suddenly she gave him a brilliant smile and patted his cheek fondly. "*Dearest* George! Don't look so glum. It's possible that Bernard will soon be very thankful for that betrayal."

Twenty-Eight

As she left Chadleigh House, Livy was astounded at the agitation of her feelings. Why, she asked herself, should she become so upset merely because she'd seen George kneeling beside a lovely young woman? She herself had no designs on him. The very idea of it was ridiculous. Even though he'd kissed her once in a moment of weakness, he did not think of her as an object of desire. She was like a maiden aunt to him—a maiden aunt whom he'd grown fond of, perhaps, but no more than that. She'd known that from the first. Therefore, why should she be cast down, when he was showing a perfectly normal interest in a woman his own age? Or was she even younger? Livy had not actually caught a good look at the girl. She wondered why the girl was weeping, but truly it was no business of hers.

She entered Leyton House, hoping to get to her room unseen. Once there, she would be free to—what? Throw herself on the bed and weep? That would be an utterly jingle-brained indulgence. Quite beneath a woman of her mature age and sensible disposition. So she was half pleased when Kelby approached and informed her that Lord and Lady Leyton were expecting her to join them for tea. There would be no weeping just yet.

She handed Kelby her cloak and bonnet and went down the hall to the sitting room. To her surprise, there was another guest having tea with them. "Look who's come especially to see you," Felicia greeted.

It was Horace Thomsett. He immediately put down his cup, got to his feet, and came across the room toward her. Livy remembered him as being a too-stout, overbearing bore, but the man coming toward her seemed different. In the country, he'd always appeared to be stuffed uncomfortably into his hunting clothes or evening attire, his face red and his manner uneasy, as if he were out of place. Here in town, however, wearing a well-cut, dark blue coat and a tastefully striped gray waistcoat, he looked impressive and self-confident. "Good afternoon, Miss Henshaw," he said, lifting her hand to his lips, "I've been so eager for a chance to see you again."

"We've been chatting about his brother's betrothal," Felicia said as Horace led Livy to a chair. "Horace tells me that the happy couple is quite excited about my dinner party."

"You must give your brother my congratulations," Livy said.

"You can tell him yourself, at the party," Felicia chirped happily. "Beatrice and Algy getting married! I can't believe it actually came about. And to think that it was all my doing!"

"All your doing, indeed," Leyton sneered. "What a boastful creature you are, my love! Taking credit for the workings of fate. As if all that's required to make a match is to ask some couples to come for a visit."

"Very well, then, I won't claim full credit for it," Felicia said, calmly pouring a cup of tea for Livy, "but you can't deny I played a part. Here, Horace, be a dear and pass this teacup to Livy."

Horace handed Livy the cup. "I didn't come here today to talk about Algy's betrothal," he said to her quietly. "I came to ask you to let me take you up tomorrow afternoon for a spin in my curricle. You are a stranger in London, I understand, and it would give me pleasure to show you some of the points of interest."

"How very kind of you," Livy said, smiling at him. "Thank you. I'd be delighted."

Very pleased with himself for having accomplished his

mission with success, Horace stood up and made a bow to his hostess. "I'll be off, then. Thank you, Felicia, for a delightful tea. I look forward to your dinner party. And, Miss Henshaw, I shall be here at two, if that is agreeable."

"Yes, quite agreeable," she assured him.

He started out of the room just as Kelby appeared in the doorway, with a rumpled-looking George right behind him. "Lord Chadleigh, my lady," Kelby announced. "He said you'd have no objection to his coming right up."

"You *don't* have any objection to my barging in, do you, Felicia?" George asked from the doorway.

"No, of course not." His sister threw him a welcoming smile, but her expression immediately changed to surprise. "My goodness, Georgie, what are you wearing? You look positively disheveled."

George looked down at himself and realized he was still in his bespattered riding clothes. "I was riding," he mumbled, embarrassed. He'd been in so great a hurry to see Livy that he'd forgotten to change. "I'm sorry, Felicia. I've probably tracked mud all over your carpet."

"Never mind the carpet," his sister assured him. "You know that I adore you, Georgie, whatever you wear, but I would have preferred you to look more presentable when I am entertaining guests."

"Never mind the nonsense about being presentable, George, and come in," Leyton ordered.

George stepped over the threshold and found himself face-to-face with Horace. "Ah, Thomsett!" he said, startled. "How do you do?"

They shook hands. "How do y' do, Frobisher," Horace said, forcing a smile. "I was just leaving." He hoped his smile would hide his aversion to George. He was remembering that George had rivaled him for Livy's attention during the weekend at the Abbey. Wondering if George's presence would have an effect on Livy now, he cast her an uneasy glance. As he feared, she was staring—rather nervously, he thought—at the newcomer.

He decided to show the damn fellow that he'd had some success with her. "Tomorrow, then, Miss Henshaw," he called to her loudly, "at two?"

She glanced up at him. "Yes, of course," she said with what was, to him, a most satisfying smile. "At two."

George watched Horace leave, gritting his teeth. He had an aversion to Horace that equaled Horace's to him. *So,* he thought, *the stuffed prig is still trying to cozy up to Livy. I ought to kick him down the stairs!*

"Don't just stand there gaping, George," Felicia said. "Come and sit down. Will you take tea?"

"Of course he'll take tea," Leyton put in, grinning at his brother-in-law. "What else would he have come here for? Certainly not to hear you criticize his appearance."

"I didn't come for tea or for criticism," George said, nevertheless brushing some dried mud from his knees. "I came to see Livy."

Felicia looked at him suspiciously. "But I thought . . . didn't you just see her?"

"Yes, but not long enough to speak to." George crossed the room to where Livy was sitting and looked down at her. "Why did you run off so quickly?"

Livy dropped her eyes and stirred her tea. "I didn't wish to interrupt you."

"As a matter of fact," George said, taking the seat that Horace had vacated, "I would have welcomed an interruption."

"An interruption of what?" Felicia inquired curiously.

George didn't answer but looked at Livy with an upraised eyebrow, as if to challenge her to answer.

"Tell me!" Felicia insisted.

"Yes, tell her," George said, keeping his eyes on Livy's face.

Livy glared at him. "Very well, since you insist, I shall. Your brother, Felicia, was making an offer to a young lady."

George hooted. "An *offer?*"

"Well, you were on your knees!"

"Goodness!" Felicia exclaimed, rising from her chair so abruptly that she almost overturned the tea cart. "I don't believe it. Georgie, is this true? Are you smitten with someone at last?"

George threw his sister a look of disgust. "I was on my knees consoling Harriet."

"Oh, is that all." Felicia sat down again, thoroughly disappointed. "Harriet is always crying on George's shoulder," she explained to Livy.

"Harriet?" Livy couldn't resist asking.

"Harriet Renwood," Leyton promptly informed her. "She has a tendre for George's best friend."

"Oh," Livy said in a small, shamed voice.

"Yes, oh!" George mocked. "Jumping to conclusions on insufficient evidence is like skating on thin ice. More often than not one ends up thoroughly drenched. But enough of this roundaboutation. I want to know just what was it you came to see me about."

"Well, it was *not* to cry on your shoulder about being rejected in love," Livy retorted.

"I'm very glad to hear it. Then what was it?"

Leyton, who'd been observing these two guests closely, cleared his throat. "I just remembered, Felicia, that I . . . er . . . have a letter to show you in my study."

Felicia, who'd found the conversation fascinating, did not like the interruption. "Letter?" she asked. "What letter?"

"You know the one." Her husband winked at her. "That letter I mentioned at breakfast. Do come along. I'm sure Livy and your brother will excuse us."

"*Oh!*" Felicia's eyes widened. "Yes. Yes, of course." And with a quick glance at her brother and her friend, she hurried out of the room on her husband's arm.

As soon as they were alone, George asked Livy again why she'd called on him.

"It was to thank you," Livy said.

"Thank me? Good God, whatever for?"

"For the tongue-lashing you gave to my uncle."

To George, this was completely unexpected. "You want to thank me for *that*? I thought you'd wish to tear my eyes out!"

"I might have, except that whatever it was you said to him worked a miracle." She'd been sitting stiffly in her chair, feeling defensive and tense, but she now softened, warming to her subject. "You'd never believe the change in him, George. It's improved the lives of everyone at the castle."

"How?" George wanted to know. "What has he done?"

"For one thing, he's enlarged the staff. He had McTavish hire two footmen, and Mrs. Nicol was permitted to take on an upstairs maid and a kitchen maid. Can you believe it?"

"Well, well, well!" George sat back, stretched out his booted legs, clasped his hands behind his head, and grinned with self-satisfaction. "Amazing! I never would have guessed that a few insulting words—honest, perhaps, but insulting—would have such an effect."

"Neither would I," she said.

George basked in glory for a moment, but then another question occurred to him. "But what has the old curmudgeon done for *you*?" he asked.

"That is the most amazing part. He's been treating me like a veritable princess. You must tell me, George, what you said to him about me."

"I don't quite remember. The words just poured out of me extempore. I think I said that he's been treating you like a bond slave."

"A bond slave?" She smiled and shook her head. "That was putting it a bit strongly, wasn't it?"

"Not strongly enough, if you ask me."

Livy grew thoughtful. "I suppose he's now trying to make up for it. The more I think about the change in him, the more amazed I am. Do you know what he gave me when I left for London? *Two hundred pounds,* merely for spending money! I've never had more than a couple of pounds in my hands at one time. And now I have two hundred!"

George grinned. "From a tightfisted Scotsman, I suppose two hundred pounds is a veritable fortune."

"It's a fortune wherever it comes from! And if you don't think so, you must be wealthier than I imagine. In any case, you can now understand why I had to thank you."

He studied her speculatively. "Does this mean you are in my debt?"

This was unexpected. "In your debt?"

"Yes. I did something for you, therefore shouldn't you do something for me?"

"Good heavens, George," she exclaimed, shocked, "are you asking for a *reward*?"

"Yes, I suppose I am," he said, grinning. "Not in a material sense, of course. I have no designs on your two hundred pounds."

"I didn't think you did. Asking for a reward is not what I would have expected of you, George."

"No? Why not?"

"Because I know you didn't do the deed in the hope of being rewarded. You just said it was an extemporaneous act. You didn't plan it, so you couldn't have anticipated a reward."

"Perhaps I didn't at the time," he said with a wicked leer, "but I intend to take advantage of it now."

She shook her head in smiling disapproval. "What sort of reward did you have in mind?"

He shrugged. "Nothing very costly, as rewards go. Something simple, like agreeing to go riding with me, for example."

She stiffened. "No, I'm sorry, George. That reward is too costly for me."

"Going riding with me is too costly?" The amused gleam in his eyes died at once. "Are you saying that the thought of going riding with me is so repugnant that it can't be considered even as a small thank you?"

She lowered her eyes but did not answer.

"But evidently you are perfectly willing to go riding with Horace, isn't that so?" he accused.

She rose from her chair, the epitome of offended dignity. "Horace did not request my company as a payment of a debt," she said in a voice from which all the warmth of a moment ago was gone.

"Damnation, Livy, the debt business was a joke, and you know it."

"Then I need not consider your invitation seriously."

"Of course you should. My phrasing may have been unfortunate, but my desire to take you riding is perfectly sincere."

"And so is my refusal."

"But why?" Bewildered, he got to his feet and grasped her shoulders. "You can't pretend you prefer Horace's company to mine. I've seen you with him. You barely tolerate him."

"My feelings for Horace, or for anyone else," she said icily, throwing off his hold on her, "are not your affair."

"Dash it, Livy," he swore in frustration, "why can I never get you to soften toward me? Why does every one of our encounters, no matter how well they start, end in this kind of . . . of cold dismissal?"

She turned away from him, nonplussed. She'd meant to thank him, not to quarrel. "I don't . . ." she began. "I didn't mean to—"

"Georgie," came Felicia's voice from the doorway, "will you stay to dine?"

"No," George said sourly, throwing Livy one last look and stalking to the door, "I don't think I'm wanted."

Twenty-Nine

*L*eyton was asleep, but Felicia lay beside him wide awake and staring at the reflection of the firelight flickering on the ceiling. "I don't believe it," she said aloud.

"Hmmmm?" Leyton tried not to wake up. He pulled the comforter up over his ears and turned on his side, away from her.

"I said I don't believe it," Felicia repeated, loud enough this time to indicate that she expected a response.

Leyton burrowed into his pillow. "Mmmm," was his sleepy response.

"Montague Leyton," his wife snapped, "I'm trying to speak to you!"

Leyton sighed. When his wife addressed him with his given name, he knew his goose was cooked. "What don't y' b'lieve?" he muttered sleepily.

"That George cares for her. It's not possible."

" 'S very possible," Leyton said, still hoping to avoid a confrontation. "Go t' sleep."

"How can I sleep when you make me fear that my brother has lost his mind?"

Leyton sighed again and gave up. "I never said he'd lost his mind," he declared, sitting up and rubbing his eyes to wake himself properly.

"But you said you thought he was taken with Livy." Felicia turned to her husband worriedly. "Doesn't that mean he's lost his mind?"

"Not at all. Livy is a lovely woman. Why shouldn't he care for her?"

"Good God, Leyton, she's eight years older than he! It's unheard of!"

"It's unusual, I admit, but there's no law against it. Besides, do you think, when I first looked at you, that I said to myself, 'Ah, she's two years younger than I, so I'll fall in love with her?' "

Felicia giggled. "What *did* you think when you first looked at me?" she asked, sitting up and snuggling into his shoulder.

"I thought," Leyton said, kissing her forehead, " 'That young lady over there is wearing the most ridiculous hat I ever saw.' "

"Oh, fiddle!" Felicia slapped him playfully on his shoulder. "Tell me really."

Leyton, recollecting the moment, smiled in the darkness. "You were talking to one of my old school chums when I first saw you. Laughing with him in the most natural way, not in the least put off by his being on crutches. I thought you beautiful and charming and kind, and I immediately decided to marry you. If I could manage to win you, of course."

"Is that true? You decided at first glance that you wanted to marry me?"

"Yes. And I didn't care a whit how old you were."

Felicia grew thoughtful. "But, dearest, Livy is *thirty-five*. She's well past the flush of youth. Why should George choose her, when he could have his choice of any young beauty in London?"

"He's had that choice for years, hasn't he? Yet he hasn't chosen any one of them."

"That's true. I've often wondered why. I told myself that he wasn't ready to settle down."

"Perhaps he just hadn't met the right woman," Leyton suggested.

"And you think Livy is the right woman?"

"I think George thinks it."

Felicia, her brow knotted, moved away from him.

"You said a moment ago that Livy is lovely. But I had the impression that men found her plain. Sort of . . . spinsterish."

"Horace doesn't seem to find her so. And neither does your brother."

Felicia looked at him closely. "And neither do you, evidently."

"No, I don't. I think she has a lovely face. A bit chiseled, perhaps, at the cheekbones, but interesting and intelligent and brightened by a pair of very speaking eyes. It's a face one doesn't forget."

"Does one forget mine?" Felicia asked in a small voice.

Leyton frowned at her. "That's a silly question, my love, and quite beneath you. To me, your face is perfect. But I can't speak for others. Every man sees differently, according to his nature."

Felicia, chastened, snuggled back into his shoulder. "So it's perfectly possible that George is in love with Livy," she said in pensive acceptance. "But that means that I now have to wonder if Livy is in love with him."

"That, dearest, is another problem altogether, and if you'll forgive me for pointing it out, none of our affair. However, since I'm now wide awake, perhaps you might consider dealing with our own love affair." With that, he pulled her back down with him under the covers, thus bringing the discussion to a very satisfactory conclusion.

Thirty

Horace was convinced that his outing with Livy had been a very successful affair. With a winter sun shining softly through a thin veil of clouds, the day had been pleasant enough for a leisurely drive through Hyde Park. A number of his acquaintances, all well dressed and prosperous-looking, had passed by and greeted him cordially, making him believe that Livy must have been impressed by his apparent popularity and importance. By the time he brought her home, he was quite pleased with himself.

Livy, however, had not found the afternoon as pleasant as he. She did not like to admit it, but she'd found his company tedious. He was humorless, self-important, and excessively formal. Even his manner of addressing her was pompous. Although she'd invited him to call her Livy, he'd insisted that such informality was not properly respectful. "I'd be honored to call you Miss Olivia, if you'll permit it," he'd compromised. With such a man, carrying on a conversation was a strain. By the time she'd said good-bye and hurried into the house, she was relieved to be free of him.

Felicia, who'd been watching for her, greeted her at the door. "Come and have some tea with me," she insisted. "I want to hear all about your drive."

By the time Kelby brought in the tea and a platter of assorted tea sandwiches, Livy had given her friend all the details of the ride through the park. Felicia poured the tea in silence, dredging up the courage to tackle the subject that she and Leyton had discussed the night before. As she handed her friend the cup, she took a breath and asked, "Do you like him?"

"Horace?" Livy gave an indifferent shrug. "Yes, I suppose so."

"Enough to wish him to pursue you?"

Livy glanced up at Felicia curiously. "Are you asking the question because you want me to wish it?"

"I ask it because I want you to be happy."

Livy stirred her tea. "Horace is not the sort to make me happy, Felicia," she answered frankly.

"Good. I didn't think he was. You deserve someone more special." She pretended an intent interest in choosing a sandwich while she remarked casually, "Someone like George."

"*George?*" Livy felt her cup rattle in the saucer. "Whatever has George to do with me?"

"Leyton thinks he may have a tendre for you."

"For *me?*" She couldn't believe her ears. "Whatever gave him such a ridiculous idea?"

"I don't know. But the idea is not so ridiculous."

"It is. Utterly ridiculous."

Felicia, beginning to suspect that her friend was denying her true feelings, inched her chair forward. "You know, Livy, that Leyton is very perceptive about people. Very perceptive."

Livy tried to steady her hand. "I think he's missed the mark this time."

Felicia sat back again and crossed her arms over her chest. "Your hand is shaking," she pointed out.

Livy gulped. "I know." She set down the cup and saucer as if they were burning her fingers.

"Are you in love with my brother, dearest?" Felicia asked. The question was blunt, but her voice was tenderly sympathetic.

The sympathy in Felicia's tone undid Livy. She covered her face with her hands. "Yes, more fool I," she admitted tearfully.

"Don't say that. My brother is very lovable."

"Yes, he is. But not a good match for a thirty-five-year-old spinster."

"Leyton says that men don't ask a woman's age when they fall in love."

Livy lowered her hand and wiped her eyes. "That may be, but if he's speaking of George, he's quite wrong."

"Why do you say that? How can you be so sure of how he feels? If Leyton believes George cares for you, he must have seen some signs of it. Even I've noticed how he singled you out at the Abbey and how he enjoyed engaging you in conversation. And you yourself told me that he stood up for you with your uncle."

"All that is true. He likes me. I, too, was confused by his attentions at first. But you know your brother. He is good-natured and warm to everyone. And he does like me. He does! As a man would like a . . . a maiden aunt!"

"A maiden aunt?" Felicia was appalled. "Good God!"

The response disappointed Livy. Felicia's expression indicated shock but not disbelief. Livy had hoped that Felicia would argue the matter; that she'd say, *No, Livy, you're quite wrong. My brother, good-natured as he is, would not go to such lengths to please a maiden aunt.* But Felicia did not say that. She did not try to convince Livy that she was wrong. In fact, the opposite had happened: she, Livy, had convinced Felicia that she was right. "Yes, a m-maiden aunt," she said miserably, covering her face again to hide the tears that began to drip from her eyes. "Someone toward whom he f-feels k-kindly and p-protective and even f-fond. But th-that's all."

Felicia was indeed convinced. Her good-natured brother probably did like Livy, but liking was a far cry from loving. As much as she would have liked to believe that her brother could fall in love with her best friend, it was unlikely. That he admired her and was fond of her, yes, but there was probably not more to it than that.

Felicia, looking across the tea table to where Livy was trying pathetically to hide her tears, felt a rush of sympathy. Livy was a wonderful, admirable, lovely woman and deserved to be married. It wasn't fair! Breaking into empathetic tears, Felicia rose from her chair and knelt beside her friend. "Don't c-cry, dearest, p-please don't cry," she urged, taking Livy's hand. "Perhaps we sh-shouldn't write Horace off. He's really a g-good man. Do you think you might f-find it in your heart to t-take to him after all?"

Thirty-One

"*Bernard has the idea that you paraded your friends before him in order to pass him on to one of them.*" Harriet brooded over those words all night. By morning she believed she fully understood their significance. She dressed and went down to breakfast, her course of action completely determined. She said nothing to her mother about her plans, but as soon as she could do so without being noticed, she slipped out of the house and strode quickly down the few streets between her house and Bernard's rooms in Providence Court.

Pratkin, of course, heard her come in and ran to bar her way. "He's not seeing visitors today," he told her, trying to reach the foot of the stairway before her.

But Harriet, two decades younger than he and therefore more agile, reached it first and started up the stairs. "He's awake and dressed, I hope," she called down over her shoulder, "because whether he is or not, Pratkin, old dear, I'm going up to see him."

Harriet threw open the door to Bernard's study with a bang and stormed into the room. Bernard, who was seated at his desk going over some papers, looked up, startled. "Harriet!" he exclaimed with an alarmed shudder.

"How dared you!" she said with melodramatic intensity. "How *dared* you!"

He blinked at her uncertainly for a moment and then wheeled his chair away from the desk to confront her. "I don't blame you," he said. "I've regretted it ever since. It was rude."

The words made no sense to her. "What? What was rude?"

"You didn't deserve it. I'm very sorry. It was just that I was startled at seeing you."

Harriet shook her head in confusion. "I don't know what you're—"

Pratkin stuck his head in at that moment, breathless from his climb up the stairs. "Sorry, sir, she didn't let me stop 'er. Shall I escort 'er down?"

"No, of course not," Bernard said impatiently. "Go away."

"Yes, Pratkin, go away," Harriet echoed.

Pratkin flicked a glance from one to the other, broke into a grin, and hastily backed out.

"Where were we?" Harriet asked, rubbing her forehead nervously.

"I was apologizing for my rudeness."

"Oh, yes. But I don't know what you're talking about, Bernard."

"I'm speaking of the scene on the street yesterday. When I cut you."

"Oh, that." Harriet dismissed it with a shrug.

It was now Bernard's turn to be confused. "Is that not what's made you furious?"

"No, not anymore, though I admit to having been quite perturbed at the time."

"Of course you were." He lowered his head. "I've been feeling ashamed of myself ever since."

"And rightly so. But that's not why I'm here. And it's not why I'm furious." She glared down at him, arms akimbo. "Why did you assume that I introduced you to my friends in order to pass you off to one of them?"

He stared at her for a moment, trying to determine what this was all about. "Did George tell you that?" he asked.

"Never mind that. Answer my question."

"I'll wring his damned neck!"

"I'll wring yours, if you don't answer me."

He shrugged. "What else was I to think when you had your friends parade their charms before me so blatantly?"

"There's a great deal 'else' you could have considered. For instance, if that had been my purpose, why would I first have suggested that you sit out the dancing with my brother?"

"Oh," Bernard said, bemused, "I hadn't thought of that."

"Yes, *oh!* And you could also have considered that my behavior in coming here and begging you to attend the ball was certainly peculiar for someone who was trying to pass you off on someone else."

"Not necessarily," he said defensively. "It's not peculiar behavior for someone who had always gone out of her way to be kind to me."

"*Kind?* I never believed, Bernard, that you could be such a fool!" Exasperated, she flounced across the room and threw herself upon the sofa.

He wheeled himself after her. "Did you march up here, brazenly unchaperoned, just to tell me that you *weren't* trying to pass me off onto one of your friends?"

"Yes, you idiot, that's exactly what I've come to tell you. And to ask you, if passing you off was *not* my motive, then what could that motive have been?"

"I suppose you're telling me that your motive was just what you said it was—a way of helping me to enjoy the ball. Only that and nothing more. An act of simple kindness."

"Kindness, *again?*" She glared at him. "You mean that my motive was to be kind to a crippled man, is that it?"

He met her angry gaze with one of his own. "Isn't it? Let's have the truth for once."

"Dash it, Bernard," she cried impatiently, "try not to be so stubbornly blind. Surely you can see that to have thrown myself at you as much as I have is a great deal more than mere kindness. Only a nun could be as kind as all that!"

Her true meaning broke upon him like a physical blow to the brain. His eyes widened in utter disbelief. "What are you saying? You can't be trying to tell me . . ." His voice broke, and he turned the chair away from her. "You *can't* be!"

"Why can't I?" She got up, came up behind him, and put her arms about his neck. "Is it so hard to believe I love you?"

He sat unmoving for a moment, basking in the delightful sensation of feeling her arms about him, while he let her words sink in. Then he took hold of one of her arms and pulled her round to face him. "Look at me, Harriet," he said softly.

She knelt beside the chair and gazed up at him. "I'm looking," she said.

"You know how much I love you. But you're too wonderful to settle for only a part of a man. You deserve more than this."

"You sound like my mother. She knows that I had made up my mind long ago to have you, but she keeps warning me that life with you will be difficult."

"She's probably right."

"No, she isn't. My life with you will be happier than it's ever been." She laid her head down on his knee. "You are more a man to me than any I've known," she said in a tremulous whisper. "You can do everything and anything I need a man to do."

Expelling a long sigh of pure joy, he bent down and lifted her up onto his lap. She slipped her arms about him tightly and gave him a long, lingering kiss. When at last they paused for breath, he smiled down at her. "There's one thing I can't do, you know," he reminded her. "I can't dance."

She smiled back. "That's all right, my love. When I have a desire to dance, I'll send one of my friends to sit it out with you."

Thirty-Two

$\mathcal{A}$ proper dinner party, Felicia believed, required at least ten at table. And for this occasion, she decided that it would be a charmingly sentimental plan to invite everyone who'd been present at the Abbey when Beatrice and Algy met. "The problem," she said when she discussed the matter with Leyton, "is that the Stonehams are traveling abroad, and that leaves only eight of the original assemblage: the bridal couple, Horace, George, Livy, Elaine, and us."

"Mmm," murmured Leyton, who was engrossed in the *Times*.

"Are you listening to me, Leyton? We must have another couple to make ten, but most of our friends have not yet come to town." She paced about the sitting room thoughtfully. "We could ask the Crowells, I suppose, but he likes to dominate the conversation, and she has an unfortunate tendency to belch."

Leyton had heard enough to realize he did not want the Crowells. "Ask Bernard and Harriet," he suggested promptly.

"But, dearest, didn't you hear what George said about them? They aren't speaking."

"Exactly why I suggested them. Neither of them need know the other is coming. Then, when they come face-to-face, they may make it up. You'll be doing a good deed."

Doing a good deed was very appealing to the sweet-natured Felicia. Eight invitations were sent out that very day.

Dinner invitations were not extraordinary occurrences to any of the recipients, but in this case each of them reacted to the invitation as if the occasion were indeed extraordinary. Each had a personal reason for wishing to attend, and each immediately set about preparing for it. Beatrice wasted no time in calling on the most modish dressmaking establishment in Leicester Square and ordering a new gown. Algy sat down at his desk and tried to compose a witty response to the congratulatory toast he knew would be made. Horace, who'd been working hard at losing weight in order to advance his cause with Livy, ordered his valet to take in one inch from the sides of his favorite evening coat. Elaine sought the advice of her mother, her aunt, and three of her best friends on which of her dozens of evening dresses would be most fetching to the male eye. George, after eliciting a promise from his sister to seat him next to her house guest, spent a great deal of thought on the problem of how he might charm, cajole, or hoodwink Livy into liking him a little. Even Livy, who was expending just as much effort to steel herself against any temptation to soften toward him, nevertheless paid a visit to Felicia's modiste and spent almost all of her two hundred pounds on a new gown— a wine-colored Florentine silk with full sleeves and a lovely flounce at the bottom.

Harriet and Bernard were the only recipients who considered refusing the invitation. When Harriet received hers, she went immediately to see Bernard. She found him frowning over his. "I think that at least one of us must refuse," he said after they'd exchanged an affectionate greeting.

"Why?" Harriet wanted to know.

"Because the party is to celebrate Beatrice Rossiter's betrothal to that Thomsett fellow. If we revealed the news about our engagement, it would infringe on the honor due to theirs."

"But we needn't tell them about ours," Harriet pointed out. "Besides, Mama doesn't want us to tell anyone until she makes her own party to announce it."

Bernard laughed. "Anyone seeing me look at you would know at once that I'm top-over-tail for you."

"I suppose my face reveals it, too," Harriet agreed. She slid onto his lap and snuggled happily into his embrace. "It's hard to hide the fact that it's midsummer moon with us."

"Although," Bernard mused, "it might be fun to try."

"Try what?"

"Try to pretend we're still at odds." He lifted her chin and grinned down at her. "Even George doesn't yet know about us. We could go to the party and act cold to one another. Speak to each other in icy monosyllables. Never address one another directly, and never offer the other even a tiny smile. Do you think you could play the role?"

Harriet giggled at the prospect. "I think I could. But only if you promise not to look at me too much."

So they, too, sent Felicia their acceptances. Felicia reported to Leyton that she was very pleased with the responses. Not one invitation had been refused. She might have been much less pleased had she guessed how charged with undercurrents her little dinner party would be.

Thirty-Three

*T*he party began in a perfectly ordinary way, with the guests gathering in the drawing room for preprandial drinks and conversation. Felicia, Leyton, and Livy were on hand to greet each one. The first to arrive was Horace, who took Livy aside as soon as he had his drink in hand. "You look lovely," he murmured, lifting her hand to his lips, "and charmingly daring in that striking red gown."

Livy wondered if "charmingly daring" meant that the dress was too bold for a woman of her age. But Felicia had assured her that London ladies wore gowns a great deal bolder than hers. And Felicia herself was resplendent in a dandelion-yellow satin gown and a sequined, feathered headdress that could not be called modest. So Livy told herself to put the word "daring" out of her mind.

Bernard arrived with George, and they soon drew Leyton into a lively discussion of a procedural reform that was soon to be debated in Parliament. George, however, managed to take a long look at Livy, who was standing before the fireplace with a wineglass in her hand. Regally graceful, in an elegant red gown, with her hair pinned up and only a few small curls framing her face, she was a perfect subject for a master portraitist. George found himself wondering, for the thousandth time, why he had ever found her spinsterish.

The betrothed couple arrived next and were greeted

with a round of cheers and congratulations. Then Elaine breezed in, her velvet cloak (which she should have handed to a footman downstairs) floating out behind her. She removed it with a flourish and handed it to Kelby, thus dramatically revealing a breathtaking gown of blue brocaded silk with so pronounced a décolletage that the room fell silent for a moment. It was, Elaine thought, as if the very air had gasped. Preening, she did not consider the possibility that the gasp signified shock rather than admiration. She smiled and told herself that this was going to be a delightful evening.

Harriet came in shortly afterward, shy and a bit nervous, in a demure gown of tearose pink crape. Bernard had a hard time pretending not to notice her. He would have liked to say to George, "Isn't she a rose-colored vision?" but of course he had to restrain himself. Felicia, noting the girl's uneasiness, immediately put an arm about her. "I know many of my guests are strangers to you," she said, "but you'll soon feel quite at home." She promptly introduced Harriet to all the ladies, starting with the bride-to-be and ending with Livy. By some mutual instinct, neither Harriet nor Livy acknowledged that they recognized each other. They both understood that the embarrassing moment in George's library was best forgotten.

Harriet had taken a quick look at Bernard when she'd first stepped into the room, but she'd not yet had to face him. When at last Felicia brought her to the corner where the three parliamentarians were gathered, Harriet steeled herself for the critical moment to come. "This is my husband, Leyton," Felicia said, "and of course you know George and Bernard."

"How do you do, Lord Leyton?" Harriet said, offering her hand to him. She then smiled at George, but merely nodded coolly to Bernard and turned away. *Oh, well done, my love!* Bernard said to himself proudly.

Meanwhile, Elaine was using the time to flirt with every man in the room, one after the other, including her host and the groom-to-be, but saving George for last.

She brazenly sidled up to him and, detaching him from the others by hooking her arm into his, asked in a soft, cooing voice if he would escort her in to dinner.

"It will be my honor," he answered without returning her smile. His manner was polite and pleasant, but inside he was seething. Escorting Elaine Whitmore in to dinner was not at all what he'd planned, but the manner of her request had trapped him. *I'm caught,* he thought, *but I'll be damned if I stand here and let her flicker her lashes at me.* In desperation he tried to find a way to escape. He glanced down at the glass he was holding; fortunately he hadn't yet taken a sip. "But first, if you will excuse me, I must deliver this drink," he said and bowed himself away.

He brought the drink directly to Livy, uncomfortably aware that Elaine was watching. Livy was seated on a sofa with Horace, but George had no choice but to barge in. "Here's your drink, Miss Henshaw," he said loudly, trying, with a wink and a slight movement of his head in Elaine's direction, to indicate he needed her assistance. Desperately.

"My drink?" Livy glanced in the direction he'd indicated, saw Elaine staring at them, and understood. "Oh, yes, thank you," she said, quite willing to help him out of his difficulty. "Won't you join us, my lord?" She patted the place beside her in spite of Horace's obvious irritation at this intrusion. George, with a smile of gratitude, sat right down.

Livy wondered why she'd aided him. Here it was, just the start of the evening, and by inviting him to sit, she'd already weakened her resolve. Of course, she'd only done it to help him avoid the predatory Elaine. She would have done the same for any needy nephew. And to prove to herself that she had *some* character, she would refrain from giving the needy nephew any further attention. Therefore, she simply turned away from him to Horace, soothing that neglected swain by telling him how much she'd enjoyed their outing in the park the day before.

Soon dinner was announced. Elaine promptly appeared in front of the sofa to claim her escort. George got to his feet and offered his arm. As they moved across the room toward the dining room, Bernard, who happened to be just in front of them, stumbled on a small bump in the carpet. Harriet, not very far behind, gave a loud gasp and rushed forward. George, however, had already caught his friend's arm and kept him from falling. "Don't worry, Harriet," he assured the frightened girl, "he's fine."

Harriet, embarrassed at the thought that she'd given the game away, felt her cheeks grow hot, but Bernard realized that everyone else in the room had been alarmed as well and had therefore not taken particular notice of Harriet's reaction. He lowered his hand and felt for hers. He managed to grasp it and, hiding it in the folds of her skirt, gave it a reassuring squeeze. That was enough to restore her confidence. "I'm not in the least worried," she said to George with exaggerated indifference, tossing her head and turning away.

Elaine leaned happily on George's arm as the assemblage moved decorously to the dining room, pleased that he, being of the highest rank in this group, was expected to lead the parade. But this was his sister's house, and a small, informal party, and George had no intention of being first. Instead, stepping aside and bowing to Algy, he passed the honor over to the bridegroom-to-be. Algy, proudly leading his bride-to-be, marched with appropriate dignity into the dining room at the head of the line.

Once inside, Elaine was doomed to a second disappointment. She'd assumed that since George was her escort, he'd therefore be seated beside her at the table, but this, too, was not to happen. Felicia had prepared a seating plan with great care. There was to be promiscuous seating: Beatrice, Horace, Livy, and George on Leyton's right, and Algy, Harriet, Bernard, and Elaine on his left, with Felicia herself at the foot. No mistake would be made, for gold-edged place cards were prominently displayed at each setting.

Elaine found her card at Felicia's end of the table, with Bernard next to her. George's place was opposite, but Elaine could see at once that it would be almost impossible to carry on a conversation with him across so wide a space and over such a dismaying array of glasses, candlesticks, and flowers. George, on Felicia's left, had no such disappointment, for as Felicia had promised, Livy was right beside him on his left. However, with Horace seated on her other side, George knew he had his work cut out for him.

Bernard also realized there were difficulties ahead. Felicia had put Harriet on his right and Elaine at his left. Conversing with Harriet was, of course, taboo, and conversing with a shallow, narcissistic creature like Elaine would surely make him feel like an awkward schoolboy. He'd accepted Felicia's invitation thinking the game he'd concocted with Harriet would be fun, but now he wondered if he'd made a huge mistake.

When everyone was seated, Leyton tapped on a wineglass for attention. As two footmen circled the table filling glasses with champagne, he smiled down at the betrothed couple and lifted his glass. "Beatrice, Algy, my wife tells me that it behooves me to say a few wise words about the happiness that awaits you in your wedded life. I regret that I have no wise words. Nothing that anyone can tell you about wedded life can truly prepare you for it." Here he cast a mischievous glance at his wife, who retorted by sticking her tongue out at him. "Marriage," he went on, serenely unperturbed, "is like a forest, with all sorts of surprises lurking behind the trees. I can only pray that your good sense and good natures will guide you through. May you have joy in the great adventure you are about to undertake. Ladies and gentlemen, raise your glasses. Here's to Beatrice and Algy."

The others got to their feet, echoed those last words, and downed their champagne. Algy then rose, unfolded

a paper he'd removed from his breast pocket, and rea‹
aloud the speech he'd prepared. It was a flowery enco›
mium about his great good fortune in having been ac
cepted by the world's most beautiful and charmin‹
woman and his unworthiness to be so rewarded. Not onl›
was his lack of spontaneity ludicrous, but the perfor
mance was so stodgy and pompous that George had dif
ficulty in restraining a laugh. He looked across a
Bernard, whom he knew would share his amusement, bu‹
to his surprise discovered that Bernard was exchangin‹
an amused glance with Harriet. At that moment they di‹
not seem to be at odds. *Is it possible,* George asked him
self, *that they've so suddenly made up their quarrel?*

With the ceremonial duties done, Felicia signaled fo‹
the first course to be served. Usually at this point th‹
table would be alive with conversation and laughter, bu‹
Felicia noted that the atmosphere seemed strangely sub
dued. Horace was speaking rather loudly to Livy, bu‹
otherwise all was silence.

To the hostess's dismay, this constrained atmospher‹
continued through the soup course and the two course‹
following. Harriet tried to converse with Algy, but afte‹
congratulating him on his little speech, she could not fin‹
a subject that appeared to interest him. Elaine tried t‹
flirt with Bernard, but she could not get him to look u‹
from his plate no matter how many times she made ‹
half-round turn to give him a proper glimpse of he‹
bountiful gifts. What was worse, George, too, was re
fraining from sending glances at those gifts from acros‹
the table. Elaine was not accustomed to such inattention
In order to pour balm on her wounded feelings, she kep‹
signaling the footman stationed behind her to refill he‹
champagne goblet. At least the *footman's* eyes poppe‹
whenever he bent over her.

Even Horace was finding it difficult to keep up a con
versation with Livy; it seemed to him that her mind wa‹
somewhere far away. George was just as unsuccessful i‹
getting her attention. He'd tried several times to speak
to her, but she invariably put him off with a dismissiv‹

monosyllable. In between rejections, he kept an eye on
Harriet and Bernard, to see if he could verify his impression of their reconciliation. But there was never a repeat
of that intimate glance. They both sat in stony silence,
neither acknowledging the other's existence. After a
while, George began to wonder if that glance between
them had been nothing more than a product of his
own imagination.

The atmosphere brightened when the main entree was
served. It was *Agneau de la Maintenant,* grilled lamb
slices redolent with herbs and smothered in shallot gravy.
The fragrance that permeated the air was delectable
enough to lift the most flagging of spirits. Felicia took
hope. Perhaps it needed nothing more than good food
to save a dinner party from the doldrums.

George tried once more to persuade Livy to speak to
him. He had one ace up his sleeve and decided this was
the time to play it. He leaned over to her and whispered
in her ear, "I've decided, ma'am, to lower the cost of
repaying that debt you owe me."

She looked up at him in surprise. "What debt?"

"You know very well what debt. Didn't you yourself
admit that the effect of my scolding of your uncle put
you in my debt?"

She sighed and put down her fork. "I told you I was
grateful. Very grateful." Dropping her eyes from his, she
added softly, "I know I'm in your debt, George. You've
always been kind to me. Too kind."

"Then return the kindness," he responded promptly.
"Pay off your debt to me."

"But a truly good deed, my lord, should be done from
the heart, not in the hope of a selfish reward," she
pointed out. "Your wishing to be paid contaminates the
deed. It makes the doing of it far less noble."

He would not let her shame him. "I agree. I am not
noble."

"I won't believe you lack nobility," she insisted.

"But I do. And I wish to be paid. I'm offering you a
bargain, my girl. I will make the payment easy. You

needn't go riding with me if you don't wish to. All you need do is to talk to me. Right now. Is that too ignoble an offer?"

She couldn't help considering the offer. Though she'd made a pledge to herself to keep him at a distance, she asked herself if it would be a very great compromise of that pledge to talk to him a bit. *No, not very,* she answered herself, *if I'm careful not to let the exchange go too far.* "Very well, I'll accept your offer," she said, "because I do not enjoy being indebted to anyone. But if I do as you ask, will that be the last payment I have to make?"

"Yes, on my word of honor."

"Well, then," she prompted, bracing herself, "what is it you want to talk about?"

He sat back in his chair and crossed his arms over his chest. "I want to know why you don't like me."

Her eyes widened. She hadn't expected such bluntness. "But I do like you, George," she said.

"No, you don't. You won't go riding with me, though you did with that lumpish clod sitting next to you, and I know you don't really like him."

She frowned at him in disgust. "In the first place, you have no way of knowing whether I like him or not. And, incidentally, I do not approve of you calling him a lumpish clod. And in the second place, I can like you whether I go out riding with you or not."

"No you can't. If you truly like me, what reason can there be for you to refuse to go with me?"

She had to smile. "The answer, my dear, can be found in this silly conversation. You sound like a spoilt little boy, whining, 'You gave *him* a sugar tart, but not *me!*' I like that little boy, truly I do, the way a maiden aunt likes a charming but spoilt nephew. But I don't have to go riding with him."

George's face fell. "Is *that* what I am to you?" he asked, appalled. "A spoilt little nephew?"

She patted his hand, auntlike. "A spoilt, charming nephew. Whom I quite like."

She was making sport of him, but he felt as if she'd given him a blow to the solar plexus. He lowered his head and sat there, stunned.

Livy was surprised at what seemed to her a strange reaction—she'd expected him to laugh. But she couldn't dwell on it. She had to respond to Horace, who'd been insistently tapping on her shoulder. *It seems the conversation is over,* she said to herself ruefully as she turned away. *My debt is paid.*

Meanwhile, Elaine had been watching George shower the attention she so deeply craved on a dowdy spinster who, she believed, had not an iota of her looks and charm. To assuage her feelings of offended self-esteem, she'd been having her champagne glass repeatedly refilled. She was now quite cast away. Waving her champagne glass unsteadily, she leaned toward Bernard. "You have t'admit," she said, breathing into his face drunkenly, "that I'm a gool deed . . . a *good deal* prettier than 'er!"

Poor Bernard leaned back in his chair to get as far away from her as he could, but she only leaned closer. "Don' y' think I'm a gool deed prettier?" she demanded, still waving her glass about. She was almost on top of him, her barely clad breasts pressing against his chest. He flung out an arm to free himself, hitting her outstretched arm. Her glass flew out of her hand and fell into Harriet's lap.

Harriet gave a little scream and jumped up. Bernard, horrified, shoved Elaine from his chest, crying out, "Harriet, dearest, I'm so sorry!" Elaine, meanwhile, fell upon the table, her shoulder plopping into Bernard's platter of half-eaten, generously sauced *Agneau de la Maintenant.*

While Harriet uselessly brushed away at the skirt of her gown, Elaine managed to get to her feet, but it took her a moment to get her balance. Not so foxed that she was unaware of the sea of faces gaping at her, she nevertheless ignored them. It was more important to examine the sogginess she felt on the shoulder of her gown. What she saw almost sobered her. Globs of thick, brown liquid, dotted here and there with bubblets of shallot, slithered from her shoulder down front and back, one rivulet slowly making its way into the cleavage of her breasts. Drunk as she was, she knew it was her life's worst moment. In a last, desperate attempt to regain some semblance of dignity, she straightened up, lifted her chin, and glared at the stricken Felicia. "You, my once dear friend," she announced with the thick, forced clarity of a drunkard trying to prove his sobriety, "seem t' have a talent for s'lecting th' mos' boring fellows t' dine with. This 's defina'ly the *worst* dinner party I ever 'tended." And in a hopeless attempt to flounce, she staggered out of the room.

But George didn't watch her. Having, by sheer force of will, thrust his own troubles to the back of his mind, he was staring at another scene unfolding across the table. Harriet was bending over Bernard, each of them assuring the other that the incident had caused no real damage. The look in their eyes was unmistakable. "Bernard, you sly dog," George crowed in delight, "is there something you haven't been telling me?"

Thirty-Four

With various expressions of shock and dismay, six of the party watched Elaine take her churlish departure, but George's shout across the table caused an abrupt shift in their attention. All eyes turned immediately to Bernard and Harriet. There they were, arms about each other, caught in a frozen moment of concerned affection. The couple had no choice but to admit their betrothal.

The announcement was greeted with universal delight. The air was suddenly filled with merriment. Everyone embraced, everyone delivered spontaneous toasts, everyone basked in the glow of the happiness that could now freely shine from the lovers' eyes. Good wishes and champagne flowed in unrestricted abundance. Even Algy and Beatrice, whom the party was intended to honor, were happy to share their celebration. Beatrice, with a sweet show of generosity, enhanced the gaiety by playing and singing a lively rendition of Harriet's favorite song, "How Sweet in the Woodlands." The party that the departed guest had called the "worst" had become, to Felicia's relief, one of the most joyful.

The celebrants did not disperse until the wee hours. Most of them fell into instant and contented slumber. Three of them did not. One was Horace, who had found the evening frustrating. He was happy for his brother, of course, but it was irritating that Algy was approaching the married state ahead of him. He was fond of Algy, but he, Horace, was the older, the wealthier, and, in his view, the handsomer of the two. True, he was a bit hefty, but he was taller and stronger than Algy by far, and his hairline had not shown the slightest inclination to recede, as Algy's had. It seemed an unfair stroke of fate that Algy was betrothed before him.

Beatrice Rossiter was, in Horace's view, a bit addle-brained, although a perfectly suitable choice for Algy. He himself preferred a more sensible, well-grounded woman like Livy. He'd had an eye on Livy from the first. She was neither young nor a great beauty, but there was something striking in her appearance. He liked to look at her. What was even more important, she had dignity and presence, could speak cleverly on almost any subject, and she would make an excellent impression on his friends and on his banking associates. He had intended to court her in a proper, leisurely style, but perhaps he should not wait. *What would be the purpose in waiting?* he asked himself. A woman in her position would surely accept him as readily now as later. With that decided, he turned himself over on his side and shut his eyes. His last thought before sleep overtook him was that he would make the offer to her the very next day.

Livy also found sleep hard to come by, but Horace had nothing to do with her wakefulness. It was George, of course, who interfered with her peace of mind. She reviewed their brief dinner conversation over and over in her mind, but she could not interpret it properly no matter how carefully she analyzed it. There was no question that she'd hurt him when she'd said she liked him as she would a charming nephew. But why was he hurt? Was it just that he was offended at what he felt was a disparaging view of him? Or was he hoping for more affection from her? If one thought about it objectively, one would have to ask why he should care what she thought of him, unless . . . But she didn't want to think of the "unless . . ." She was a scrawny old maid, eight years his senior. Any romantic thoughts were completely inappropriate. With that definitely decided, she buried her head into her pillow and waited in miserable impatience for sleep to come.

The third sleepless party guest was George himself. When he tumbled into bed, he noticed that his emotions were in an unusual state of agitation. He tossed about on his rumpled bed hour after hour, unable to settle down. He tried to calm himself by concentrating on Bernard's good fortune. He'd hoped for so long that Bernard would find happiness that he could hardly believe his wish had come true. The only troublesome thing about it, he realized guiltily, was that when he discovered that they'd come to such a happy understanding, he'd unwittingly given away their secret. Bernard might very well be annoyed with him for it. But their friendship was too deep and of too long-standing to be seriously harmed by an unwitting blunder. Bernard would get over it. The important thing was that Bernard was to wed the girl of his dreams.

Unfortunately, George had been struck with Livy's rejection on the very same evening he'd learned Bernard's good news. He tried to put the memory of it out of his mind, so that he could be free to savor Bernard's happiness. But Livy's evaluation of him—that he was nothing but a spoilt nephew to her—kept echoing in his brain. It clouded his joy. It was a drop of ink in the pure water of his delight in Bernard's triumph. The only thing that might calm him was to push all thoughts of Livy firmly out of his mind. He'd concentrate on the happy outcome of Bernard and Harriet's romance. *At least some of us,* he thought with a touch of bitterness, *are sleeping well tonight.*

Thirty-Five

*D*uring breakfast the next morning, Kelby brought in a note and handed it to Livy. "The messenger is awaiting a response," he said.

Livy glanced at the front of the sealed paper. "It's from Horace," she said in answer to the curious expressions on the faces of both Felicia and Leyton. She broke the seal and read it quickly. "Oh, dear," she sighed when she'd finished. "Must I?"

"Must you what, my love?" Felicia inquired.

Livy read the missive aloud:

> *Dear Miss Olivia,*
> *Not having had an opportunity to converse with you properly at last night's celebration, I most sincerely request the honor of your company this afternoon for a ride in Hyde Park. I am quite impatient to discuss with you a matter of great import, so I beg that you will not put me off.*
>
> *Yours, H. Thomsett.*

"I wonder what matter of import he wants to discuss," Leyton remarked, buttering his toast.

Felicia, remembering her private conversation with Livy on the subject of Horace Thomsett, looked across the table at her friend with sympathy. "I know you don't wish to go," she said softly, "but perhaps you should."

"Certainly you should," Leyton agreed heartily, being in complete ignorance of Livy's feelings. "Horace is no fool. If he says it's important, it must be."

"Very well then, I shall," Livy said reluctantly. "In any case, the weather is fine for a drive." She turned to the butler. "If you please, Kelby, tell the messenger to inform Mr. Thomsett that I shall be ready at two."

The weather, however, did not stay fine. By afternoon the sky was overcast and the wind had turned gusty, thus exacerbating Livy's reluctance to go. But, having given her word, she dressed in a warm pelisse, tied on her bonnet with a sturdy ribbon, and let Horace help her up on his curricle with as cheerful a smile as she could summon up.

Horace was handling the reins himself. Though a liveried tiger hung on to the rear, there was no one within hearing distance. The fact that Horace had dispensed with a coachman made Livy wonder why the "matter of import" required such strict privacy.

It didn't take long for Horace to launch into the subject. "I've been trying for several days to bring up a certain subject for your consideration, Miss Olivia, but . . ." He opened his mouth to proceed but suddenly hesitated.

"Yes?" she prompted.

He flicked the reins and threw her a sidelong glance. "Do you know, Miss Olivia, that I am forty-three years old?"

"Are you?"

"It may come as a surprise to you that after all these years of bachelorhood, I have suddenly taken an interest in wedlock," he said, not looking at her. "And it came about when meeting you."

Good God, she thought, *the man does not intend to offer for me, does he? It can't be!* "Indeed?" she asked carefully.

He glanced at her again. "You may find it an odd notion," he said.

"Odd?"

"Well, yes. If I may be blunt, Miss Olivia, you are a woman who has for some years put aside the intention of marrying, as I had. That both of us postponed wedlock until now is what makes the circumstances odd." He steered the carriage off the path and pulled the horses to a stop. Then, with a deep breath, he turned on the seat to face her. "I have to admit, Miss Olivia, that I hadn't been in your company for five minutes before I realized that you were not the ordinary sort of—how shall I put this?—unmarried woman of a certain age."

"You may say the word 'spinster,' Horace," Livy said with a laugh. "That is what I am."

"But not the typical sort," he assured her. "Not at all. And this opinion I have of you has been strengthened by each of our subsequent meetings. Which is why, since both of us are of an age past the foolishness of youth, I have emboldened myself to ask you—"

She cut him off with a movement of her hand. She'd pushed aside her first instinct that she was about to receive a marriage proposal, convinced that it could not be true. Now, apparently, it was. She had to stop him before the matter became painful. "Not all youth is foolish, Horace," she said gently. "I may be past the age to think of wedlock, but I assure you that there are many young women of marriageable age who would be happy to accept you."

"But the young women you speak of do not interest me. I suppose we both are of such depth of character that the young persons we meet seem immature and shallow, is that not so?"

"In some cases, perhaps, but—"

"It was when I had the good fortune to converse with you at Leyton Abbey that I began to appreciate the—how shall I put it?—"

"The depth of my character?" she supplied dryly.

"Yes." Warming to his subject, he reached for her

hand. "I realize, Miss Olivia, that you do not know me well, but I assure you that there isn't a member of my club who wouldn't vouch for my character. And I have much to offer a woman. I can claim, in all modesty, that I am quite well to pass. I have an estate in Derbyshire, where I also own a bank, I have a house here in town and a solid footing in the funds. My income is better than five thousand."

"Is it, indeed?" she murmured, trying to withdraw her hand. It was an awkward moment. Though she couldn't refuse an offer that hadn't actually been made, it was clear the fellow was on his way to declaring himself. Livy wanted desperately to stop him before he did. "But, Horace, I don't think—" she began.

Instead of releasing her hand, he grasped the other one. "I know you find this unexpected, Miss Olivia, but I'm asking you to marry me." He smiled down at her benignly. "I think we suit very well."

Livy did not reveal by so much as the twitch of her lips that she'd felt an urge to giggle. She'd had two offers of marriage in her youth, both of which had been embarrassingly romantic. One had strewn an armload of flowers over her, and the other, on bended knee, had bombarded her with flowery words. She'd considered both excessive, but they'd both been infinitely more appealing than this pompous proposition. It was as if Horace were offering her a partnership in his bank! "Thank you, Horace," she said, firmly pulling her hands from his grasp, "but I am not interested in wedlock."

Horace, having convinced himself that his offer was too splendid to be refused, especially by a woman who was past her last hopes, merely continued to smile. "I hope you're not playing coy, my dear."

"At my age it is not fitting to 'play coy,' " she assured him firmly.

Her tone could not be mistaken. She was refusing him. He could hardly believe what he had heard. "Then you are seriously refusing me?" he asked in astonishment.

"Yes. Quite seriously."

"That cannot be!" he insisted. "Forgive me for my candor, my dear, but the fact is that all women are interested in wedlock, and women of your age are even more so."

"Well, as you suggested, perhaps I am odd. I'm very sorry."

Believing her at last, he stiffened in fury. "This may very well be your last offer, you know."

"I'm sure it will be." Her voice was calm and without the slightest hint that she was offended by his aspersion. But she couldn't help thinking it ironic, if not very amusing, that Horace's supposedly flattering offer of wedlock contained some very unflattering comments. He'd described her—quite repeatedly and in a variety of ways—as a spinster past her last hopes. She would have liked to laugh off his contemptuous comments, except that they were all too true.

Horace picked up the reins and set the horses back on the path. They rode for a while in a mortifying silence. Livy was wondering if she should attempt some casual conversation to ease the tension when Horace expelled a strange-sounding, angry guffaw. "If you believe that George Frobisher will come up to scratch, Miss Henshaw," he sneered in tight-lipped petulance, "you're only fooling yourself. He has his pick of the London belles. He's only leading you on."

"I think, Horace," Livy said quietly, "that you've said quite enough. Please take me home."

Thirty-Six

$\mathcal{A}$t the same time that Livy was receiving a marriage offer, George was deciding it was time to pay a call on Bernard. He'd not had a private moment with his friend since he'd heard the good news, and he knew Bernard had much to tell him. Besides, he had to apologize for his blunder of the night before.

Bernard was expecting him. The moment George walked in the door, Bernard hobbled over to him and, leaning on one crutch, gave him a fervent embrace with his one free arm. "I was going to tell you about the betrothal today, truly I was," he swore, "no matter how much Lady Renwood would disapprove."

"Does she know I gave the game away last night?" George asked as he went for Bernard's wheelchair.

Bernard shrugged. "I suppose Harriet's told her by now. But neither of us cares if she disapproves." He sat down on his chair and grinned up at his friend. "We had a grand come-out last night and enjoyed it to the hilt. Lady Renwood's party can only be an anticlimax."

"I'm glad of that. I was afraid I'd pushed you into hot water."

"Not at all. I think Harriet and I really *wanted* to be discovered."

George, relieved of the necessity of making an apology, sat down and stretched out his legs. "Then, with that matter dispensed with," he said, "I feel free to ask the question I've held back since I learned the news."

"What question?"

"You know what question. Damnation, man, it was just a few days before that Harriet came to me in tears, complaining that you'd snubbed her in the street. How on earth did everything change so suddenly?"

"It was you, you clunch. You revealed to her how I felt about that blasted ball, did you not?"

"Yes, but—"

"It made her realize I'd completely misunderstood her motives, and she marched in here to set me straight. Well, one thing led to another and"—Bernard smiled at the recollection of what had happened next—"and here we are."

"Not so fast, old fellow, not so fast," George ordered. "I'd suggested a dozen times that you may have misunderstood her motives, but I couldn't change your stubborn mind. How did Harriet manage it?"

"It was simple, really. When I accused her of doing it out of kindness toward a crippled man, she merely said that she is not as kind as all that."

George's brow knit. "That's all? 'I'm not as kind as all that' was enough to convince you?"

"Yes, it was. If she'd not acted out of kindness, there had to be something more. And what more could there be? It was her way of telling me she loved me without actually saying it."

George nodded thoughtfully. "Of course. I see. Kindness alone would not have been enough for you."

"No, you don't see," Bernard said. "Kindness alone would have been completely inadequate." He gave his friend a level look. "In my case, George, kindness is akin to pity. When one wants love, pity—or kindness, if you will—is an insult. Can you understand that?"

"I'm not sure," George replied, rubbing his forehead. He was remembering another voice, saying, *You've always been kind to me, George. Too kind.* Somehow that memory made it seem urgent for him to fully understand. Was there a connection between what Bernard was telling him and what Livy had said?

After leaving Bernard, he went home and sat brooding in his study. He did understand why Bernard had rejected any sign of pity from the woman he loved. Bernard was crippled, but he didn't want people to see only that when they looked at him. If they were kind to him, he probably felt that his impairment was all they were seeing. To be a friend—and, even more, to be a lover—one had to see far beyond that. Anyone can make himself feel kindness to someone who needs it. But one can't make himself feel love. Love has to come on its own.

But how did this apply to Livy? *You have always been kind to me, George. Too kind.* Was Livy rejecting that kindness, as Bernard had? That was the question he had to answer. If the answer was yes, it would mean she wanted more from him. Love? And if she wanted it, did it mean that she felt love for him? How could that be, if she looked on him as a spoilt nephew?

She couldn't love him. It wasn't possible. She'd never shown him the slightest sign. Of course, there was *one* moment when . . . Just recalling it was enough to stir his blood. He'd kissed her once. He'd kissed her, and he'd felt her respond. She'd returned his kiss with real feeling. He was not such a fool or a coxcomb that he'd imagined more than was really there. He couldn't be mistaken about her reaction. Could he?

But a kiss was only a kiss. Even if he was right about her reaction, it could only have been a momentary weakness. He had no evidence at all that she loved him. She'd told him she thought of him as a mere child.

Hours went by as the questions went round and round in his brain. By nightfall, he was desperate for answers, and the only way he could get them was from Livy herself. He would simply ask her. He would tell her, as Harriet had told Bernard, that he was not as kind as she thought. And, before she could answer, he would kiss her. He'd kiss her as he never kissed a woman before. And then he'd know.

He ran all the way. He arrived at Leyton House breathless and disheveled, and burst into the dining room where Felicia and Leyton were having their dinner. No one else was at the table. "Where's Livy?" he demanded without preamble.

"Good God, Georgie, what's the matter?" Felicia asked, startled.

"Sit down, George, and have some dinner," Leyton said cheerfully. "This chicken is delicious."

George gave an impatient shake of his head. "Where's Livy, I said!"

"She's gone," Leyton said.

"What do you mean, gone?"

"You know what gone means, man," Leyton teased, nevertheless keeping a pitying eye on his brother-in-law. "Not here. Away. Flown the coop."

"Damnation, she can't be gone!" George ran a hand through his hair. It was a gesture of desperation. "Gone where?"

"Back home," Felicia said. "To Scotland."

Thirty-Seven

$\mathcal{F}$elicia got to her feet and stared at the door that George had just slammed behind him. She didn't understand what had passed. When she'd announced that Livy had returned home, her brother had gaped at her stupidly for a moment, as if he didn't understand plain English, and then he'd blinked, turned on his heel, and stormed out. "What on earth's the matter with him?" she asked in utter perplexity.

"I've told you what's the matter," Leyton said patiently. "Love is the matter. Do sit down, woman, and eat your dinner. The chicken's getting cold."

Felicia sat. "Do you truly believe he loves her?" she asked, picking up her fork but showing no indication of wanting to use it. "Livy thinks not."

"Really?" Leyton asked curiously. "Did you discuss the matter with her?"

"Yes, I did."

He raised an accusing eyebrow. "You never told me."

"I was told in confidence."

"What does that matter? I'm your husband. I thought you didn't keep secrets from me."

"I don't keep *my* secrets from you," she explained, "but I'm under no obligation to tell you my friends' secrets."

"Ha! As if you women can ever keep secrets."

"Evidently, I kept this one," she retorted proudly.

He shrugged. "Therefore you don't intend to tell me why Livy thinks George doesn't care for her?"

"No, I don't."

"Very well, then, let's drop the subject. Eat your chicken."

Felicia put down her fork. "But if you're convinced he cares for her," she said, vacillating, "then Livy may be mistaken."

Her husband made no response but calmly continued to chew his food.

"Say something," his wife demanded irritably.

"What can I say?" Leyton asked with irksome nonchalance. "I haven't enough information to comment on the matter."

Felicia squirmed in her chair, her face revealing her inner conflict. "If I give you the information, then you'll accuse me of not keeping a secret."

"It will be the truth, won't it?"

"You, Montague Leyton, can sometimes be the most irritating man in the world."

"Please pass the gravy," was all he said.

Felicia gave a surrendering sigh. "She thinks George is only being kind to her," she divulged guiltily, "but feels nothing stronger. She says he treats her like a maiden aunt he's fond of."

Leyton gave a snorting laugh "Maiden aunt, eh? That's interesting."

"In what way interesting?"

"Don't you see? George doesn't see her as a maiden aunt any more than you or I do. Livy believes it only because she sees *herself* that way."

"Oh! Yes, that *is* interesting." Felicia thought it over for a moment. "Then George must go and tell her he doesn't! At once!"

"To Scotland?"

"Yes. Don't you think he should?"

"Yes, I suppose so."

"Then, Leyton, my love, you should go at once and tell him so."

"My dear wife," Leyton said pompously, returning his

attention to his food, "as you should know after ten years of marriage, I make it a rule not to interfere in other people's affairs, especially their love affairs."

"But this is George's affair we're speaking of! That rule cannot apply to George!"

"If you feel so strongly, tell him yourself."

"I can't do that," she exclaimed, shocked. "I'd be betraying a confidence!"

He looked across the table at her with indulgent scorn. "But I would not?"

"No, of course not. She didn't tell it to *you*. Please, Leyton, you must go at once."

He put down his fork and got to his feet. "Your logic, my dear, is impeccable. So impeccable I can find no answer for it." He came round the table and kissed her. "Against my better judgment, I'll go. But if George breaks my jaw with his very effective left hook, you'll have only yourself to blame."

Leyton, wrapped warmly in his greatcoat and with his beaver set snugly on his head, hurried down the windy street toward Chadleigh House. He'd not gone far when he spied someone some yards ahead of him on the next street. He wasn't sure it was George, for the fellow was hatless, his shoulders slumped, his hands deep in his pockets, and his gait too slow. But when he passed under a streetlamp, Leyton recognized him. "George!" he shouted. "Hold on there!"

George turned, recognized his brother-in-law, and waited. Leyton sprinted over the short distance between them. When he'd caught up with him, George asked in concern, "Is something amiss?"

"No, no. But let me catch my breath." Leyton leaned against the lamppost. It took a few moments before he could go on. "I know it's not my business, George," he said when his breathing became steady, "and I won't blame you if you find you must plant me a facer with your fives, but"—he glanced uneasily at George's puzzled face—"but I've come out to talk to you about Livy."

George's face grew even more puzzled. "What about Livy? Hasn't she gone to Scotland after all?"

"Oh, yes. She's gone. Left this morning."

"Then what—?"

"Felicia thinks—no, *I* think—that you should go after her."

George squinted at his brother-in-law in the dim light. "You dashed out in this wind just to tell me this? On my meddling sister's orders no doubt."

"It may be meddling, but we—I—think it should be said."

"That I should go after her. To Scotland."

"Yes."

"Why?" George demanded.

"Don't play games, George. To make her an offer, of course."

"You think I ought to chase the woman to Scotland and make her an offer?"

"Well, yes." Leyton peered at him in sudden perplexity. "That was what you came to the house this evening to do, wasn't it?"

"How on earth did you decide that?"

"I'm not a fool, George. I've seen the way you look at her."

George groaned ruefully. "I'm as obvious as all that, am I?" he mumbled, shamefaced.

"Not to everyone," Leyton assured him. "Most people would assume that you'd prefer younger, more blatantly pretty women."

George nodded. "I assumed that myself, before I learned better. Strange, isn't it, Leyton, how someone's outer appearance changes in one's eyes when the inner person becomes known? Take Elaine Whitmore, for example. It's hard for me to imagine, now that I've become acquainted with her self-loving character, how I ever could have found her beautiful. With Livy, it's just the opposite."

Leyton smiled. "Then go to her, George," he urged. "Go at once."

"No," George sighed. "It would be a fool's errand. She won't have me."

Leyton's face fell. "Why do you say that?"

"With good reason. She thinks of me as a spoilt child."

"But you didn't think it a fool's errand tonight, when you came to the house for that purpose," Leyton pointed out.

"Yes, that's true," George agreed, sighing hopelessly. "I thought I'd make an attempt. But if she's gone back home, it's plain there was nothing—or no one—of enough interest to keep her here."

It was now, Leyton realized, that a breach of confidence was called for. He took in a deep breath. "I have it on good authority," he said quietly, "that your chances are better than you think."

George eyed him suspiciously. "Truly? On whose authority?"

"It would be a betrayal of confidence to say," Leyton said pompously.

"Come on, man, whose? Felicia's? I don't like to say this about my sister and your wife, Leyton, but Felicia's authority is not particularly dependable."

Leyton crossed his arms over his chest in a pose of adamant refusal. He would not say more.

"You surely don't expect me to dash all the way to Scotland on such flimsy evidence," George argued.

"You must take my word, George, that my authority is dependable," was all Leyton permitted himself to say.

George began to surmise that Leyton was hinting that his "authority" was someone other than Felicia. Suddenly his eyes widened. *"Livy?"* he asked, awed. "Is your authority Livy herself? Could she have suggested to Felicia that she cares for me?"

"I can't say," Leyton insisted.

But the tiny smile on his brother-in-law's face was enough for George. "Leyton, you *brick*," he exclaimed, clasping him about the shoulders and pounding his back with affectionate enthusiasm, "I don't know how to thank you! Bless you and Felicia, too. You can tell her that, for once, I forgive her meddling. Even if there's the slightest chance for me, I'm game. I'm off for Scotland this very night."

Leyton watched as George sped off down the street. He knew he'd betrayed Livy's confidence, but remembering how George's eyes had become aglow with hope at what he, Leyton, had revealed, he forgave himself. *Yes, I've betrayed you, Livy, I know,* he said to himself, *but if a small betrayal leads to a great happiness, perhaps you will forgive me, too.*

Thirty-Eight

As soon as he set foot in the door, George sent for Timmy. When the little fellow appeared in his bedroom doorway, George was busily searching through his cupboard for some warm clothes. "Ye sent fer me, m'lord?" Timmy asked, rubbing his fists in his eyes.

George glanced over at him and noted that his red hair was tousled and his eyes heavy-lidded. "Sorry I wakened you," he said, tossing his warmest riding clothes on his bed, "but I have an offer for you. If you're willing to give up sleep tonight, there will be a goodly vail in it for you. And something else. That little scullery maid of yours—what was her name, Meggie?—how would you like to see her again?"

Timmy's eyes widened. "Are ye speakin' of that Scottish poppet, Peggy?"

"That I am."

"Ye don' mean to say, m'lord, that yer goin' back to Lockerbie!"

"I am," George said as he began to strip off his evening clothes.

"Tonight?"

"As soon as the carriage is ready. It will be another race without stopping, I'm afraid, but at least there's no snow this time." He paused in his undressing and grinned at the young fellow. "It was an ordeal, last time, I admit. You don't have to go if you don't wish to. I can take the coachman."

Timmy grinned back. "Nothin' I'd like better 'n seein' Peggy again. I'll 'ave the carriage at the door in half an hour."

George hoped that his best horses and the newly renovated phaeton would be speedy enough to more than make up for Livy's ten- or twelve-hour head start. With any luck, he'd get to Lockerbie first and be standing in the castle doorway to greet her when she arrived. But it was not to be. Instead of snow, a heavy rain began to fall before they'd driven an hour. Twice that night they became so deeply mired in mud that additional horses had to be found to pull them out. The second time it happened, George surrendered to nature's greater force and put up at an inn. Another day passed before the rain stopped, and another half day before the roads had dried off sufficiently to be considered passable. Livy had probably been settled in at home for a full day by the time he and Timmy were able to start out again.

It was late afternoon when Timmy drove the carriage onto the driveway of Henshaw Castle. A footman neither of them had ever seen came down the stairs to greet them. George left Timmy to deal with the explanations and the disposal of the carriage. Tense with impatience, he ran up the steps and into the front hall. There he stopped in astonishment. The brightly lit hall did not look the same. It was actually cheerful. McTavish was standing at the stairway, an eyebrow raised in surprise at this unexpected intrusion. Henshaw Castle did not often have guests, and certainly not at an hour he considered too late for tea and too early for dinner. But when he saw George, his face lit up. "Lord Chadleigh!" he exclaimed heartily. "How good t' see ye again! I didn't know ye were expected!"

"I'm not," George said. "I've come to see—"

"Who's that, ye say?" came a voice from the stairway. *"Chadleigh?"*

To George's chagrin, it was Sir Andrew making his way down the stairs. Dressed in a kilt and a proper coat, and leaning heavily on a gnarled but sturdy wooden cane, he was a much more formidable figure than he'd been lying in bed in a nightshirt. George went to the bottom of the stairs and watched his descent with some trepidation. "Yes, I'm Chadleigh," he said, putting out his hand. "How do you do?"

Sir Andrew ignored the proffered hand. Instead he peered closely at George's face. "So *ye're* the misleared haveril who broke into my chamber and sorted me doon."

George, deciding that his best course was to stand up to the old curmudgeon as he'd done before, looked right back at him. "Though I don't quite know what a 'misleared haveril' is—" he began.

"It's a rude half-wit," McTavish offered bravely.

"McTavish!" Sir Andrew snapped, raising his cane threateningly. "Get yerself gone!"

McTavish knew when to withdraw.

When he was gone, George grinned at the old man. "I may have been rude, sir, but I'm no half-wit. I seem to have done some good with my 'sorting ye doon.' You're looking a great deal hardier than when I saw you last. In fine fettle, I'd say." He turned away and strolled about the hallway, looking at the paintings he'd never been able to see clearly before. "And, by the way, I notice that you've permitted a good many more tapers to be lit in this hallway since I've been here. At last one can see where one is going."

"Aye, an' a pretty penny it's costing me, too," the old man grumbled. He followed George to the side of the room and pulled him round to face him. "But gie ower this blathery talk. What have ye come back for? T' gie me anither tongue-lashing?"

"No, sir. One tongue-lashing seems to have been enough. I've come to see your niece."

"Oh, ye have, have ye?" The words were spoken in a fearful growl, but George detected a gleam in the old man's eye. "If ye have a mind t' offer for her, me lad, ye'll have to have my permission first."

"If I have a mind to offer for her, it's her permission I'll need, not yours," George retorted.

"Ye'll need mine, I tell ye. She's my ward!"

"But she's of age, is she not?"

"Mmmph," was Sir Andrew's sullen response.

"But if she'll have me," George said placatingly, "I promise to come to you and ask for your approval."

" 'Twon't be necessary. She'll never take the likes o' ye."

George sighed. "You may be right about that."

The sound of footsteps on the landing above caused both their heads to turn. First a pair of slippers came into view, then petticoats under a slightly raised lilac skirt. By the time the slippers had descended another three steps, George knew who it was. He felt a painful tightening in his chest. As she came fully into their line of sight, they saw that she was in the act of fitting one of those irritating spinster caps over her tied-back hair and didn't see them. The two men watched her in silence. She was but three steps from the bottom when her uncle cleared his throat. "Livy, m'dear, y' have a caller."

She turned her head, her arms still upraised, and froze. *"George?"*

He walked to the bottom of the stairs and held out his hand for hers. As if in a dream, she let him lead her down. "You left without so much as a good-bye," he accused her softly.

Recovering her equilibrium, she slipped her hand out of his grasp. "Is that what you've come for?" she asked. "It would seem to be an enormous effort for so small a reward."

"Wheesht, me lass," her uncle chortled, "then gie him a proper reward. Kiss the lad!"

Livy turned on her uncle with a reproving frown. "I think, Uncle, that you're wanted upstairs."

"Oh, I am, am I?" Sir Andrew sneered. "Vera well, I'm off, I'm off." With a brisk swing of his cane, he turned and made for the stairway. "But if ye wish t' be private, lass, why don't ye take the wanwyt t' the sittin' room? Now that ye have fires burnin' everywhere in the house, 'twill be warm enough in there."

Livy nodded and walked ahead of George the short distance down the corridor to the sitting room. She held the door for him while he crossed the threshold, and then she turned and closed it. "There, now," she said, turning back, "what did you—?"

She was startled to find him right in front of her, so close they were almost nose to nose. Before she could step back, he pulled her to him and kissed her so fervently she was bereft of breath. She struggled against him mightily at first, to no avail. She could not even twist her mouth from his. After a few moments, she ceased the struggle and let herself relax against him. The only thing she fought against was the almost-overwhelming urge to reach up and clutch his hair.

When he let her go, she took a step back and stared at him. Unstrung, she expelled one long, startled breath. *"G-e-o-r-g-e!"*

He smiled at her. "Your uncle ordered it," he said.

She found that smile obnoxiously triumphant. "You are a cad!" she said furiously.

"But you must admit, my love, that it was not a spoilt-nephew-to-a-fond-aunt kiss, was it?"

"No, it wasn't." She tried to rub it off her mouth with the back of her hand. Then she felt herself stiffen. "Did you call me 'my love'?"

"Did I? Well, never mind. To get back to the kiss, would you call it kind?"

"Kind? I think you've lost your mind. Why would I call it kind?"

"Then by no stretch of the imagination could it be called an act of kindness toward a spinster, could it?"

She put her hand to her forehead in utter confusion. "I don't know what you're blathering about, George."

"Answer me! Did that kiss seem like an act of kindness?"

"No, I suppose not."

"Then what could the motive have been?"

"I have no idea. To show me that in addition to being autocratic and overbearing you are also libertinish?"

George didn't expect this response. It didn't follow the logic of Bernard's thinking. A wave of angry frustration swept over him. He grasped her by the shoulders, intending to shake the life out of her. But one glance at her stricken eyes melted him. "Dash it, Livy, I could wring your neck!" he muttered in desperation. "If I wished to act the libertine, would I have driven forty hours in the rain to do it? I could have stayed home, warm and dry, and entertained myself with Elaine Whitmore!"

"So you could," Livy snapped. "Then why didn't you?"

"Because, my beautiful spinster aunt, I'm not in love with Elaine Whitmore."

Livy did not move as the meaning of his words burst upon her. Then she paled, thrust off his hold, and stepped away, eyes wide with terror. "No!" she cried. "You mustn't do this!" And moving backward to the sofa, she sank down upon it and dropped her head in her hands.

He sat down beside her and took her hands from her face. "I mustn't love you?" he asked gently. "Is that what you're saying? Is there some dreadful impediment to my loving you—like a secret husband or a codicil in your uncle's will that forbids it? If there is, I'll kill the first and tear up the second."

"Don't joke about this, George," she pleaded. "You can't love me. A kiss, even an ardent one, can't change the fact that you've always looked on me as a spinsterish maiden aunt."

"Is that what you think?" He shook his head in amazement. "Do you want to know how you look to me? I find you lovely and bright and witty and charming and generous and gentle and the perfect woman for me."

She stared at him in disbelief. "I? Perfect for you? You can't mean it!"

"How can I prove to you that I do?" he asked in frustration.

"You can't." She pulled her hands from his grasp, got up, and frowned down at him. "George, I don't know what maggoty fancy has taken over your brain," she said in a trembling voice, "but please, be sensible. I'm thirty-five years old!"

"Are you indeed?" He rose and pulled her to him. "Then of course I can't possibly love you. If, on the other hand, you were thirty-three . . ."

She gave a hiccoughing little laugh.

That encouraged him. "Ah, then, you do see you've made a silly objection." Still holding her tightly, he looked down at her. "The only way I'll let you go, Livy, is if you tell me you don't love me."

She lifted her eyes to his face and studied it closely. There was nothing in his expression that was insincere. In fact, the warm glow in his eyes could not be interpreted any other way than true ardor. It made her own eyes fill with tears. "Fool that I am," she said in a choked voice, nestling her head on his chest, "I do love you, George. I do."

"Then I see no need to let you go," he said happily, and he kissed her with all the pent-up ardor she'd seen in his eyes. When at last he let her go, he took a large handkerchief from his pocket and wiped her cheeks. "Do you know, my love," he murmured, drawing her down beside him on the sofa, "that I almost can't believe I may now whisper into your ear all the love words I've been holding back for ten years?"

He drew her to him, about to embrace her again, but she lifted her head. "What did you mean, ten years?" she asked.

He pulled her back upon his chest. "Hmmm?"

"You said you loved me for ten years. What nonsense is that? We only met a couple of months ago."

"At which time you took me in immediate dislike," he murmured, pulling the spinster's cap from her head and smoothing her hair. "When did you decide you were in love with me?"

"I think I've loved you since that first day," she admitted, "when you looked at me with such aversion. That was two months ago."

"Two months, eh? You can't compare yourself to me. It's true, you know. I *have* loved you for ten years."

"Don't be silly. How can you have—?"

"When I was seventeen, I caught a glimpse of you through an open door. It was at Leyton Abbey, the weekend of Felicia's wedding party. You were rising from a hot bath, all pink and rosy. I never forgot you."

"Oh, George, really?" Quite moved, she put a hand to his cheek. "How very sweet." She let herself savor the tale for a moment before she spoke again. "But it's a long, long time since I was that girl. No wonder you looked so stricken when you saw me at Felicia's house party."

"Well, you see, I didn't get a good glimpse of your face all those years ago, and when I saw you ten years later, your face didn't match the one my boyish imagination had drawn for you." He ran a finger down the side of her face and tilted her chin up. "But I'm a man now, my love, and your face has become more beautiful to me than any other."

That required another embrace. Then he regretfully let her go and stood up. "I think we'd better go to your uncle and break the news. I only hope he doesn't send for all the new footmen to seize me by the backside and toss me out the door."

She stood up and, laughing, took his hand. "I don't think so. He likes you. Do you know, he told me once that he was certain you 'dauted' on me? I wouldn't let myself believe him."

"Then he won't make any objection to our marriage," George said, slipping an arm about her waist and starting toward the door.

"Marriage?" The word somehow surprised her. It hadn't been said before.

He stopped in his tracks and grinned down at her. "Is the idea of marriage unexpected? Surely you didn't think

I wanted you to be my doxy. You do intend to wed me, don't you?"

She nodded and buried her face in his chest. "But you do realize, George, that marriage is an . . . er . . . intimate affair?"

"Yes, so I've been given to understand."

She peeped up at him shyly. "That means you will likely see me rising from a tub again. The sight," she murmured ruefully, "may disappoint you."

"No, it won't," he assured her. "Through these bedazzled eyes, you'll always be beautiful." With arms entwined, they ambled to the door. "To tell the truth, Livy, my love," he whispered in her ear as they left the room, "there's a seventeen-year-old inside me who can't wait for the chance to leer at his Venus again."

Allison Lane

"A FORMIDABLE TALENT...
MS. LANE NEVER FAILS TO
DELIVER THE GOODS."
—*ROMANTIC TIMES*

Emily's Beau

0-451-20992-3

Emily Hughes has her sights set on one man:
Jacob Winters, Earl of Hawthorne. But her
hopes are dashed when she discovers that Jacob
is already betrothed. She will have to forget
Jacob and marry another, which is just what
she plans to do—until one moonlit kiss changes
everything.

Also Available:

Birds of a Feather   0-451-19825-5
The Purloined Papers   0-451-20604-5
Kindred Spirits   0-451-20743-2

Available wherever books are sold, or
to order call: 1-800-788-6262

S908